Chestnut Hill

All or Nothing

Also by Lauren Brooke:

Chestnut Hill
The New Class
Making Strides
Heart of Gold
Playing for Keeps
Team Spirit

.The *Heartland* series

Chestnut Hill

All or Nothing

Lauren Brooke

SCHOLASTIC

For Jonathan, Benjamin, and Daniel Chambers,
who have brought such indescribable joy into my life.

Special thanks to Elisabeth Faith

First published in the US by Scholastic Inc., 2007
This edition published in the UK by Scholastic Ltd, 2007
Scholastic Children's Books
An imprint of Scholastic Ltd
Euston House, 24 Eversholt Street
London, NW1 1DB, UK
Registered office: Westfield Road, Southam, Warwickshire, CV47 0RA
SCHOLASTIC and associated logos are trademarks and or registered
trademarks of Scholastic Inc.

Text copyright © Working Partners, 2007

The right of Lauren Brooke to be identified as the author of this work
has been asserted by her.

10 digit ISBN 1 407 10306 7
13 digit ISBN 978 1407 10306 8

British Library Cataloguing-in-Publication Data
A CIP catalogue record for this book is available from the British Library

Printed in the UK by CPI Bookmarque, Croydon, CR0 TD
Papers used by Scholastic Children's Books are made from wood grown in
sustainable forests.

1 3 5 7 9 10 8 6 4 2

This is a work of fiction. Names, characters, places, incidents and dialogues
are products of the author's imagination or are used fictitiously. Any
resemblance to actual people, living or dead, events or locales is entirely
coincidental.

www.scholastic.co.uk/zone

Chapter One

Malory pushed her sunglasses further up her nose against the glare of the midday sun. "Is someone going to let me in on the joke?" She looked across the picnic table at Dylan and Lani, who were grinning widely.

Honey paused in taking a bite out of her ham baguette. "There's a joke and I'm not in on it?"

It was Saturday morning, and Malory had joined her best friends for lunch outside the student centre.

"If you were sitting where we are you'd be able to see the funny side, too," Dylan explained, pointing at Malory's shoulder. "I take it you sneaked back down to the stables before lunch?"

Malory glanced down at her white T-shirt to see a green stain smeared over her sleeve. She groaned. Tybalt must have dribbled on her when she'd hugged him.

Lani's brown eyes danced. "You've been slimed! Maybe you shouldn't bother changing when we go over to the pool. That way you get to cool off and do your laundry in one shot!"

1

"Wasn't spending three hours with him early this morning enough for you?" Dylan teased. The girls had gone out on a beautiful trail ride that morning before the day got too hot.

Malory brushed her hand futilely over the mark left by her favourite horse. "I thought he deserved a horse cookie for jumping that tree trunk so well," she said, thinking back to the way Tybalt had just about sprouted wings to soar over the fallen pine tree.

"Admit it, you've been sneaking in practice over the cross-country course." Honey shook back the blonde hair that framed her heart-shaped face. "Tybalt didn't put a hoof wrong on the whole ride."

"I wish." Malory smiled. They were all itching to try out the new course that had recently been built on the far edge of the campus. "I never thought I'd hope for rain, but it would be so great if we could have just enough to soften the ground."

"Well, until it *does* rain we'll never be able to try out the course," Dylan said. She took a quick breath before attempting an impersonation of her aunt, Ali Carmichael, who was Director of Riding at Chestnut Hill: "I'm not risking being left with a yard full of strained tendons just in time for you girls to disappear for the summer."

"Can you believe we're finishing our first year in just three weeks?" Lani screwed up her paper napkin and pitched a perfect curveball at a nearby rubbish bin. "Wasn't it, like, yesterday that I was walking in on the rest of you in Adams?"

"Yeah, because you missed your flight," Dylan recalled. "And it took Lynsey two minutes to sink her claws into you."

A frown creased Lani's forehead as she thought back to their first night at Chestnut Hill. "Oh, yeah. Didn't she say something about bringing my steers with me instead of leaving them back home on the ranch?" Lani deliberately deepened her Southern drawl. "She thought I was a regular cowgirl."

The girls all laughed at Lani's exaggerated accent.

"You have to admit the whole Chestnut Hill experience would have been something else without Lynsey," Honey said, smiling.

"Something else is right." Dylan looked past them and her mouth dropped open. "Um, speaking of which, is there a Malibu Barbie look-alike contest that I'm not aware of?"

Malory followed Dylan's gaze. Lynsey Harrison had stepped out onto the patio and was fishing in her purse for her Calvin Klein shades. She wore an emerald sarong over a Ferrazi jeweled bikini and looked all set to take a dip in the pool. *Which is getting more and more tempting*, Malory thought, as she lifted her dark hair up on to her head to try and cool herself down. It felt like it was about one hundred degrees in the sun.

Just then, Honey's phone began to vibrate on her tray.

"It's him, isn't it?" Dylan demanded, with a wink at Malory. They all knew Honey was expecting a phone call from Josh Hartley, an eighth grader at the nearby boys' school, Saint Kits.

Honey nodded and flipped her phone open. "Hi, Josh," she said warmly. Malory was amused to notice her friend blush, even though Honey and Josh had been dating for a couple of months now.

Lynsey came to a halt at their table in time to overhear Honey suggesting she meet Josh outside a coffee shop that afternoon. "Another date?" Lynsey commented coolly, raising her eyebrows. "Maybe this time he'll get around to asking Honey to go with him to the formal."

"Can it, Lynsey," Dylan said shortly.

"Aren't you on your way to the pool for a swim?" Malory asked, hoping that Lynsey would take the hint and leave.

"And mess up my highlights?" Lynsey looked aghast, as if Malory had just suggested taking a bath in battery acid. "I'm going sun-worshipping. I'm planning on wearing a strapless vintage Chanel to the Saint Kits formal and there's no way I'll have time to visit my mother's tanning salon before then." Her voice trailed off as she looked down at Malory. Without missing a beat she pulled her shades down her nose to stare at the stained T-shirt. "Eew! What is that *fungus* on your shoulder? Didn't someone tell you we're supposed to keep our science projects in the lab?"

"Ha-ha," Dylan interjected. "How will we ever cope without your razor-sharp wit when we leave for the summer, Lynsey?" Her voice oozed sarcasm.

Lynsey brushed back her long blonde hair with a deliberate flip of her wrist. "There's no need to freak just because I don't consider Malory bringing E. coli to the table good hygiene."

"*I* don't consider coming to the table half-dressed good manners, but you don't hear me saying anything," Dylan retorted. "Don't let us hold you up; we wouldn't want you getting strap marks now. Picture that in your vintage Chanel."

Lynsey narrowed her eyes at Dylan, but sashayed away from the table, her body language clearly designed to proclaim that she'd won that particular match.

Honey snapped her mobile shut. "Did I miss anything?"

After quickly shooting a warning glance at Dylan, Malory shook her head. "So, did you set something up with Josh?"

"The bus will get us to Cheney Falls at one o'clock, so I told Josh I'd meet him outside Starbucks at two. That'll give us some time to shop for the formal first. Can you believe that it's only three weeks away? That's a twenty-one day countdown to the biggest social event on this year's calendar!" Honey grinned, breathless.

"Or, if you want to be real precise, call it five hundred and four hours," Dylan chipped in. "But the formal might have to share first place for stellar events with our end-of-year dorm party."

Malory hid a smile at Dylan's optimism. Adams House hadn't even met yet to discuss the theme for the party, although the word was that the meeting would be in two weeks. "With all this partying going on, I agree with Honey that we definitely need some retail therapy. Do you realize that thanks to the tennis tournament last weekend it's been two entire weeks since we hit the mall?"

"And a Saturday just doesn't feel complete without at least one new outfit," Lani teased. "Maybe Honey should call Josh back and tell him he's been dumped. I don't know if I can handle sharing Honey with her boyfriend on our one shopping day of the week."

"You're only saying that because you're jealous," Honey replied humourously, pretending to take a swipe at her friend.

"Hey, you're the one who's going to be recycling outfits if you keep giving up your shopping time," Lani pointed out, holding her palm up in the air and turning away from Honey. "I guess boyfriends are more important to you."

Malory didn't join in the laughter; instead she dropped her gaze down to her plate. She knew her friends were skirting around mentioning her relationship with Caleb. *Or lack of one*, she thought to herself. She fiddled with a lettuce leaf, thinking how, not long ago, she probably would have been planning a double date with Honey at the mall. *I can't believe how quickly everything's changed.*

Last summer, Malory had got to know Caleb Smith, who was, like Josh, an eighth-grader at Saint Kits. They'd spent the holiday hanging out at the same local stables before starting at their new schools. When Caleb had asked her out a few months back, Malory hadn't hesitated in saying yes. But Caleb hadn't contacted her since their fight at the end of last term. *Has he changed over the last year, or is it just that I don't know him as well as I thought?* She frowned, remembering how unfazed Caleb had been at the rumor that Ali Carmichael might be replaced. He seemed to think it was only important to have a Director of Riding who would bring home the red ribbons.

"Hey, guys," said Tanisha Appleton, one of the eighth-graders from their dorm, as she plopped a blue plastic bucket half-filled with money on to the table in front of the girls. "We're collecting for the seniors' graduation. Dig deep!"

The whole dorm, except for the seniors, had met the night before to decide on what parting gifts they would give the twelfth-graders. After ninety minutes of discussion, they settled on a great plan. Rosie Williams, a junior and a genius with a digital camera, was going to take a shot of Adams House with the sun setting behind it. Lisa Zoltowska, one of Rosie's classmates, had offered to take charge of getting prints made, and Helen Savage, a junior who was going to major in interior design at college, had offered to frame them.

Malory fished ten dollars from her purse, feeling relieved when the others put in similar amounts. She still occasionally felt self-conscious about not being as well-off as most of her classmates. She would never have been able to afford coming to Chestnut Hill if she hadn't been awarded a riding scholarship. But she never felt bitter when she listened to other people's plans for Caribbean cruises, summers in the Hamptons, and trips to Europe. Her holidays were spent exactly how she wanted: at home with her dad. In his last email he'd told her that he'd bought a recipe book of barbecue recipes for them to experiment with during the summer. He'd taken up cooking since her mom died, and he loved trying out new dishes on Malory. It might not be as glamorous as Lynsey's planned holiday to Aruba, but she was willing to bet it would be every bit as memorable.

"Was that your BlackBerry, Dyl?" Lani asked as a tiny bleep sounded.

Dylan nodded, quickly accessing the mail on the screen. She hardly ever let her parents' birthday gift out of her sight, ever hopeful that the handsome French boy she met while skiing in Aspen would text or email. "It's from Henri!" she squealed. She began to scan the mail, chuckling aloud at parts.

"No fair!" Lani protested. "Either read it out loud or read it in private, Walsh."

"OK," Dylan agreed. "But I'm stopping if I get to anything juicy."

Lani rolled her eyes. "Yeah, right. In your dreams."

"Every night, Hernandez, every night." Dylan grinned. "OK, listen to this: *Well, ma chérie*—" She broke off and clutched her hands dramatically over her chest. "Did you hear that? He called me *chérie*!"

"Come on, Dyl, what else does he say?" Malory prompted.

Dylan squinted down at her BlackBerry. *"You are probably either busy riding Morello right now or perhaps eating brunch? Do you remember the mountain of waffles we got through each morning of our holiday? I swear we ran Aspen out of them. I bet they were about to call a national waffle crisis by the end of our holiday. Speaking of crises, I'm still having nightmares about our last day. . ."* Dylan glanced up at her friends. "You know, the rest of it really isn't that interesting."

"You wanna bet?" Lani said, leaning forward.

"It sounds like you're just getting to the best part!" Honey agreed mischievously.

"You know, this would be a really good time to throw me a lifeline, Mal," Dylan appealed to her friend.

"And miss finding out why poor Henri is suffering?" Malory refused to bail out her best friend.

Dylan gave an exaggerated sigh before continuing. *"I still can't believe you insisted trying out that jump on my snowboard. Never mind, I guess you won the most novel way of how not to go over a jump! I just wish I hadn't been standing so close when you decided to bail off in midair. Still, my legs are almost back to normal and you'll be glad to hear a hot wax fixed my board."*

"Way to go, Walsh!" Lani roared with laughter.

"If *you'd* seen the drop on the other side, you'd have quit before you started!" Dylan retorted. Then she smiled dreamily. *"C'est l'amour, non?"*

Malory couldn't help admiring Dylan's confidence.

She never seemed to indulge in the soul-searching Malory was doing right now over Caleb. Dylan's ability to throw herself wholeheartedly into crushing on Henri without reservation impressed Malory. Especially since, to Malory, Henri's email sounded more like a friendly chat than anything with serious romantic undertones. Henri's father was American and his grasp of English was pretty good, so it wasn't likely to be a confusion of language that gave Malory this impression. Could Dylan be getting a bit too carried away by her rose-coloured holiday memories?

For a moment, Malory considered pointing this out to Dylan. *But what if I'm wrong? I can't say anything – with the way things are between Caleb and me, it'll just look like jealousy.* Malory crossed her fingers under the table, hoping her worries over Henri were misplaced. It was enough that she was feeling down about Caleb without Dylan joining the pity party.

Malory pushed open the glass doors and walked into the Adams dorm foyer. She'd left her friends for a few minutes to go make a phone call to her dad. She hadn't told anyone, but today was a difficult day for her. It was the second anniversary of her mom's death and she had a sudden longing to hear her dad's voice.

As she headed over the waxed hardwood floor, Malory noticed that there was an envelope sticking out of her mail pigeonhole. She didn't have a clue who could be writing to her, because she usually used email. Brimming with curiosity, she walked over and pulled the envelope out. It couldn't be from Caleb; he wouldn't use businesslike, cream-coloured stationery, or type her name and address. Her pulse quickening, Malory flipped the envelope over to read the sender's details: THE CAVENDISH RIDING FOUNDATION. The name was vaguely familiar, but Malory had no idea why they'd be writing to her.

Puzzled, she tore open the envelope and pulled out the letter.

Dear Miss O'Neil,

We are pleased to inform you that you have been short-listed for our summer riding programme, which commences on June 9. One of our representatives will be coming to watch your performance at the All Schools League Show on May 1. If you are selected for the programme, you will be given the opportunity to train and compete on this summer's A-Level circuit with the area's most talented young riders.

Please return the form attached to indicate your interest and provide full details of yourself and your horse.

May I take this opportunity to offer my congratulations and best wishes for a successful outcome.

Dr Brian Drummond

Malory caught her breath. Short-listed for the most prestigious junior riding programme in Virginia? She reread the letter another two times before she was able to process the neatly typed words.

Malory was realistic enough to know she was a good

rider – she wouldn't have been awarded the Diane Rockwell Scholarship otherwise – but she'd always been conscious that she didn't have the same polished equitation skills as most of the other girls. She didn't have an immaculate hunter seat like Lynsey, or the advantage of private riding lessons like Dylan. Instead, her strength lay in understanding what a horse was thinking and knowing how to coax the best performance out of him in particular situations. But this letter seemed to be offering Malory the chance to join the previously closed world of A-Level show-jumping. Was she really good enough for that?

With her heart pounding louder and louder, Malory reread the line *If you are selected for the programme you will be given the opportunity to train and compete on this summer's A?Level circuit with the area's most talented young riders.* The Cavendish selectors obviously thought she was good enough. With trembling hands, Malory used the envelope the letter had arrived in to fan her flushed face. She'd never dreamed that the buzz of winning a scholarship to Chestnut Hill could be matched, but this was an offer that came pretty close. She couldn't wait to see her friends' reactions. Apart from anything else, they'd be able to confirm she wasn't imagining this amazing turn of events!

Almost as if she'd summoned them, Malory's friends walked through the foyer doors a minute later.

"Mal, are you coming to get ready for the pool?" Lani called.

At a loss for words, Malory waved her friends over.

"What's up?" Dylan asked, seeing Malory's shocked expression and spotting the letter in her hand.

Malory opened and closed her mouth, aware that she was doing a good impression of a goldfish, but too stunned to speak. Instead, she handed Dylan the letter. Honey and Lani crowded around to see.

"The Cavendish Riding Foundation wants to train you for the A-Level circuit? Unreal!" Dylan exclaimed, after she had scanned the sheet of paper.

"Mal, that's brilliant – you so deserve it," Honey said excitedly.

"OK, I'm jealous," Lani declared. "You're going to have the best summer!"

"I've been short-listed, not selected," Malory pointed out, trying to stay calm.

"That's just a formality," Dylan said loyally. "You'll obviously make the cut."

"I wouldn't get too excited, Malory," Lynsey Harrison warned as she walked down the red-carpeted staircase with her friend Patience at her side. She was carrying a bottle of suntan lotion and her eyebrows were raised haughtily.

"Lynsey got a letter, too," Patience informed them as she followed Lynsey across the polished hardwood floor, the heels on her flip-flops clacking noisily. "I bet every school team rider has been sent one. Lynsey's a shoo-in to be selected, especially with Bluegrass. I don't think Malory on Shanks' pony will exactly cut it with the Cavendish Foundation."

Lani frowned. "'Shanks' pony'?"

"It means going on foot," Honey muttered.

Malory felt like she'd just had a bucket of cold water thrown all over her. It hadn't occurred to her that she'd need her *own* pony to ride if she was to get through the final selection of the Cavendish programme.

She sensed Dylan stiffen with anger beside her. "You think every school team rider has been sent out one of these letters, huh? Well, I hate to tell you, but I'm one such team rider and *I* haven't been short-listed," she said, flicking back a strand of red hair. "Gee, Patience, it must really suck being wrong all the time."

"I doubt the reserves made it onto the list. The Cavendish Foundation is looking for the best riders, not the almosts," Lynsey drawled.

"That would explain why Patience hasn't been approached," Dylan retorted. "Maybe she could loan Malory her horse for the summer. Talk about killing two birds with one stone. Malory would get to do the programme, and Minnie would get to be ridden by someone who knows her right rein from her left." Lynsey's jaw dropped, and Patience turned purple.

Malory didn't want to take part in a conversation where the knives were out so blatantly, even if Dylan was just standing up for her. And she needed to get away from Patience's and Lynsey's smug expressions. Only minutes ago, she had been thrilled about the Cavendish offer. Now it looked like it might be an impossibility. "I'm going to go change my T-shirt," she said, hurrying away before anyone could say anything.

14

Back in her room, Malory tugged her stained T-shirt over her head and tossed it into the hamper before pulling on a clean blue one. Catching a glimpse of her reflection in the mirror, she noticed her hair had gone crazy with static. She retrieved her comb from the bathroom, where she'd left it earlier, and stood at the window while she smoothed out her long dark locks.

Normally the horses would be grazing in the paddocks now, but with the weather being so hot, they were being turned out at night and kept in the barn during the day. It was odd staring out over the empty fields. Instead of seeing horses everywhere, Malory could only make out dusty brown patches in the gateways and around water troughs to show that they had been there recently.

She leaned her arms on the windowsill. The offer made by the Cavendish Foundation was an unbelievable opportunity. But, as Patience had been so quick to point out, Malory didn't have a horse to compete on. Malory tried to convince herself that she wasn't that disappointed. *Even if I did have a horse, I wouldn't stand a chance of being selected against the other candidates, who probably have a ton of A-Level competition experience. But if I'm being considered someone must think I'd fit into the programme.*

Another thought had been bothering Malory ever since she'd opened the Cavendish letter. She'd been really looking forward to spending the summer holiday with her dad. If she could somehow get around the problem of not owning her own horse and did get selected for the Cavendish programme, then her plans for getting some real quality time with her father would be lost.

Thinking about her dad made Malory remember that she'd been on her way to call him before she'd been distracted by her letter. On today of all days, she shouldn't have let it slip her mind.

"I'm sorry, Mom," Malory whispered, feeling her throat close. She felt a stab of guilt that, on the second anniversary of her mother's death, she'd spent the morning laughing with her friends. Last year, as soon as she'd got out of school, she'd raced home to her bedroom to cry the tears she'd been desperately holding back all day into her pillow. "I wish *you* were here to tell me what to do about the Cavendish Riding Programme."

With only a heartbeat's pause, her mother's voice spoke in her head as clearly as if she'd been standing alongside her: *Go for it, sweetheart. This is your chance to shine! Never forget you're my brightest star and always will be.*

Chapter Two

Malory welcomed the cool breeze that swept over her as she walked down the centre aisle of the barn. She hadn't wanted to call her dad while she was still mulling over Patience's words. Her dad would sense immediately that she was distracted and today wasn't the day for burdening him with any worries. So she'd escaped down to the stables to try and clear her thoughts.

There was no way she could afford to rent a pony for the summer, Malory reasoned as she studied the horses. And besides, she wasn't sure that was even an option.

A chorus of whickers came from the horses looking over their doors. Malory usually distributed pats and treats to the ponies in equal doses but today she hurried straight to Tybalt's stall, eager to be with him – even if it was for the third time that day!

Tybalt was watching her approach, his ears pricked forward in curiosity. But as soon as he caught her scent, he lifted his head and pulled back his upper lip, just like he was grinning. Lynsey might think she was nuts for sticking with the temperamental pony but Malory felt a connection with him that was impossible to put into words.

She pulled back the bolt on Tybalt's door and stepped inside, breathing in the smell of hay and horse. Tybalt snuffled her hand, hopeful for a treat.

"Sorry, boy, I didn't bring anything this time," Malory apologized. Tybalt stopped snuffling and quietly rested his muzzle against her shoulder.

"You'd have loved my mom," Malory whispered in Tybalt's ear. "She had this way of looking below the surface. She'd have seen how wonderful you are right from the start." She knew her mom would have been doing cartwheels over the news from the Cavendish Foundation. She'd always encouraged her daughter's passion for riding. Malory's eyes pricked with tears as she remembered when she was six and her mother had discovered her sitting bareback on her grandparents' neighbour's horse.

"Zanzibar," she murmured, flipping a section of Tybalt's mane so it lay on the right side. "When I first saw you I thought *you* were Zan, you looked so much like him." She smiled. "Mom would have taken that as a sign that you and I were meant to be together." Tybalt shifted but he didn't move away as he would have done a few months ago.

Malory paused as a thought struck her. Was it just coincidence that the letter from the Cavendish Foundation had arrived today of all days? *Maybe it's a sign that Mom will be rooting for me.* She leaned her head against Tybalt's neck and thought back to one of the very last times she had enjoyed with her mom. "I'd just won a clear round competition at the riding school, and Mom took me out for pizza to celebrate," she murmured. "We ate outside, and Mom ordered this huge ice-cream sundae for us to share. She pulled this sparkler out of her purse, stuck it in the sundae, and lit it. She'd brought it because she totally believed that I was going to win even though I thought I'd have three refusals at the first fence." Malory swallowed hard. "She was the greatest." Her fingers tightened in Tybalt's mane.

Tybalt swung his head around and nibbled at her pocket before letting out a sigh. "I know, I know," Malory smiled, stroking his nose. "While I'm dreaming of Mom, you're dreaming of a pocket full of treats." Tybalt snorted as if in agreement and Malory chuckled. If only Tybalt were hers, then she could take him with her to the riding programme. That would be awesome. The beautiful brown horse had claimed a permanent piece of her heart, no doubt about it.

"Malory?" Ali Carmichael, the Director of Riding, looked over the stall door. "I thought I heard your voice. Who were you talking to?"

Malory felt a blush creep over her face. "Um, nobody. Just Tybalt."

Ms Carmichael smiled understandingly. "Sometimes I go down to the stable block to talk to Quince. Horses make the best listeners, don't they?"

20

Malory didn't reply right away. She was too distracted by the image of Ms Carmichael sitting on an upturned pail, chatting with her gorgeous grey horse. "Why not Morello?" Malory asked, referring to Ali's other horse, the feisty paint gelding who was Dylan's favourite.

"Morello has a tendency to answer back," Ms Carmichael told her, totally straight-faced.

Malory grinned. "So *that's* why he and Dylan get along so well."

"Kindred spirits," Ali Carmichael agreed with a twinkle in her eye.

Malory decided that this was a good moment to tell her instructor about the riding programme. "I got a letter today with some big news," she began. "Have you heard of the Cavendish Foundation?"

Ms Carmichael leaned her elbows against the door, smiling again. "I've not only heard of them, I provided them with a reference for you! They're an organization that selects promising young riders to compete on the A-Level competition circuit."

Malory felt a thrill at the description. "They've short-listed me for their summer programme."

"I'm not surprised." Ali beamed. "That's great news, Malory! If you get through the final selection then I'll come root for you in some of the summer shows."

"Thanks," Malory said shyly. She wondered if she should confide in her instructor her concerns about not having her own horse for the programme.

But just as she was about to speak, Ms Carmichael

stood back and brushed some specks of sawdust off her yard jacket. "Well, I'd better go finish feeding before the horses start a mutiny."

I guess it can wait, Malory thought as she watched her instructor walk away. But she knew she didn't have too long to figure out what to do about not having her own horse for the programme. The Cavendish selectors were expecting her to send a reply about whether she wanted to keep her short-listed position.

Looking down at her watch, Malory saw that she had enough time to prepare Tybalt a spritzer. He was out of the calming spray she'd mixed for him the week before. "I'll be back soon," she promised the gelding before heading to the feed room.

The shelves above the feed bins were stacked with supplements. Malory's container of alternative remedies was at the end of one shelf, alongside a tub of cod-liver oil. She reached up for it and began to measure out grapefruit seed extract, lavender, marjoram, vetiver, and orange. When Amy Fleming, a veterinary student at Virginia Tech, had come to Chestnut Hill to help with Tybalt's problems, she'd suggested the spritzer to help soothe his nerves. Malory thought fondly of the warm, pretty college girl.

When the spritzer was ready, she grabbed a bottle of lavender oil and went back to Tybalt. The brown gelding was pulling at his hay net.

"Time for your massage," Malory announced. She tipped a few drops of lavender oil into her palm and began to rub it into his coat with slow rhythmic circles.

It was another method Amy had taught her to help Tybalt relax. Tybalt's head lowered and his ears went floppy as she continued with the T-touch. If it hadn't been for Amy's intervention, Malory doubted the pony would have kept his place at Chestnut Hill. Despite some obvious problems, Ali Carmichael had taken him on loan until he'd proven himself. Back then, he hadn't even been able to transition from a walk to a trot without breaking into a sweat. Amy had shown Malory how to help Tybalt work through his trust issues, and now he was almost unrecognizable from the way he had been when they'd found him.

"If you could talk, what would you tell me to do about finding a horse to ride?" she asked as Tybalt's munching became slower. "You'd probably tell me to work it out by myself," she guessed, knowing the gelding's feisty personality.

A few minutes later, she had worked all the way down Tybalt's neck and flank. "You're done," she told him with a pat on the neck. "I'll come by after dinner to turn you out." Helping to lead the horses down to the paddocks was one of the most special parts of the day. She loved watching them trot across the grass, tossing their heads and chasing one another. Tybalt had a favourite place to roll, and every evening he would canter over to it before dropping to the ground and creating an enormous dust cloud.

Malory gave Tybalt a hug, reluctant, as always, to go. *If I find it hard leaving Tybalt for a few hours, how am I going to cope being without him for the entire summer? At least if I don't get into to the Cavendish programme then I could still come here and see him.* It had been at the back of her mind to ask Ms Carmichael if she could come up and ride Tybalt during her holiday. She knew that the school would be using the horses for riding lessons and residential courses but there might still be an opportunity for her to drop in once or twice a week.

Malory leaned even closer into Tybalt. "There's no getting around it," she whispered. "You've turned me into a one-horse girl."

When Malory pushed open the door to her room, she found her friends waiting for her.

"You should have come to the pool, Mal," Lani told her, lounging on her bed. "The water was perfect."

"I ended up giving Tybalt his massage," Malory admitted. "And then I tried calling my dad but the line was busy."

"We already had the Tybalt factor figured," Dylan commented from her position on the windowsill.

"We took bets on whether you were going to suggest riding him into town instead of the bus." Honey smiled. She jumped up off her bed. "He's not waiting in the corridor, is he?"

"Of course not." Malory sounded indignant as Honey peeked out through the door. "Why would I bring him all the way up here when there's a perfectly good foyer for him to wait in?" She winked at Lani as she kicked off her yard shoes.

There was a quick rap on the door and Razina

Olewayo, one of their dorm mates, looked into the room. "Mal, your dad's on the phone."

Malory immediately jumped up from the bed, her heart leaping. "I'll be right there."

"Don't be long, the bus leaves in five," Dylan yelled after her.

"You got it," Malory called over her shoulder. She ran downstairs to the payphone. "Hi, Dad," she said breathlessly.

"I thought the whole point of Saturdays was to chill out. You sound like you just ran a marathon." Her father's voice sounded light with amusement.

"Razina told me it was you on the phone. You don't think I'd keep you waiting, do you?" Malory laughed.

"No, but I wouldn't want you to break a leg getting to the phone, either," her dad teased. "You sound like you could use a rest. How about I treat you to a lemonade?" Mr O'Neil went on. "I could head over right away, if you're free."

"Today?" Malory was surprised. Her dad always worked Saturdays in his shoe store.

"Do you remember I mentioned hiring some help a couple of weeks ago?"

"That was just for a Friday afternoon, wasn't it?" Her dad used the free time to do his weekly accounts.

"Well, Mark has asked if he could do some Saturday hours as well. What better way to spend my new free time than to come over and see my daughter?"

Malory twisted the phone cord around her finger. She knew it wasn't a coincidence that her dad wanted to come out to see her today.

"Are you free or do you already have plans?"

"Are you kidding? Of course I'm free," Malory said quickly. A trip into Cheney Falls didn't compare with spending time with her father – especially on the anniversary of her mom's death.

"OK, honey. I'll drive over now." Mr O Neil's voice lifted with enthusiasm.

"I'll be ready." Malory smiled before hanging up. She turned to see her friends waiting for her over by the glass entrance doors. "I'm sorry, guys, but do you mind if I take a rain check on going into town today? My dad's coming out to see me."

"No problem," said Dylan, speaking first. "Say hi to him for us."

"I will," Malory promised. "Have a great time."

Honey was smoothing her hands over the new aquamarine wraparound skirt that she'd been saving for her date with Josh.

"He'll love it," Malory assured her, sensing her friend was a little nervous.

Honey smiled self-consciously. "Thanks, Mal. I wish you could split yourself in two and come with us."

"Me, too. But you'd better run or you'll miss the bus." Malory waved her friends out the door. She couldn't help feeling a little relieved that she was avoiding going to the mall. If Caleb had been at Starbucks with Josh she would have felt really awkward. The last thing she wanted was to be missing out on fun stuff with her friends to avoid bumping into

Caleb, but whenever she thought about him she felt sad – never mind how she would feel if they came face-to-face. *At least if I find a way to accept the Cavendish offer and get into the programme, then I could avoid Caleb for the holiday.*

Then it occurred to her that Caleb might have received an offer, too. Wouldn't that be just her luck?

"Why can't life just be simple?" she wondered aloud. At least spending the afternoon with her dad would be. She was looking forward to some normalcy.

Malory decided to wait for her dad in the cool of the Adams foyer. She picked up an equine magazine from a coffee table and relaxed into one of the armchairs that were placed next to the huge glass windows. With everyone out of the dorm for the trip to the mall, the room was remarkably calm and quiet.

She had just finished reading an article on lateral aids when she spotted a familiar figure in a white shirt and jeans heading up the steps to the front door.

"Dad!" Malory tossed the magazine aside and rushed to give her dad a hug.

"Hello, sweetheart." He hugged her close and she breathed in his aftershave, feeling a strange mixture of joy and homesickness sweep over her.

"I'm so glad you could come out today," she murmured into his shoulder.

She felt her dad's arms tighten around her. "I've been thinking about you all morning and wondering if you were okay." He didn't say anything further but his brown eyes were dark with emotion as he released her.

"Mr O'Neil. It's great to see you again." Ms Herson, the lower school housemother, appeared at the top of the steps. "How are you?"

Malory watched her dad smooth down his curly dark hair before shaking hands with Ms Herson. Then Malory took her dad to the student centre to get a cold drink. After getting juices from the dispenser, Malory suggested they walk down to the lake, one of her favourite places on campus.

"This place is amazing," Mr O'Neil said appreciatively when they reached the neat oval of clear blue water. Geraniums and petunias had been planted around the edge, making the shallows bright with colour. A dragonfly hovered just a couple of feet away from them before darting away to skim close to the water's surface.

"I should have brought some bread," Malory's dad said as a group of ducks swam towards them quacking noisily.

"Don't be fooled by their starving expressions. They're fed every day," Malory told him.

"How does a duck look starving?" her dad teased. "You're just like your mom, reading human emotions into animals. Do you remember that chicken that used to follow her everywhere?"

"Martha." Malory laughed as she pictured the large red hen. She leaned back on the grass and propped herself up on one elbow to face her father. "One of the reasons I love coming here is because it makes me feel closer to Mom. She would have loved this place."

Her dad stared across to the island in the middle of the lake. "She'd have wanted to swim out there," he murmured. "She just loved water. I took her out on a boat the day I proposed to her. There was a swan and cygnets paddling nearby and the sun was dappling through an overhanging tree onto your mom's face."

Malory closed her eyes, picturing the scene that she had heard described so many times. In her imagination, her mom was smiling, her long dark hair tumbling over her shoulders as she leaned forward to throw her arms around Malory's dad. "Mom told me she practically tipped the boat."

Mr O'Neil nodded. "The ring almost went overboard." For a moment a sad look crossed his face, but then he sat up and straightened his shoulders, as if taking control of his emotions. "We should rent a rowboat this summer," he suggested. "I'm going to offer Mark extra hours so you and I can spend some time together. I might even let you persuade me to get on a horse to go for a trail ride."

"That would be fantastic," Malory murmured truthfully, but her stomach twisted. How could she tell her dad about the Cavendish programme, which, if she got in, would take her away from him for the summer? Her dad's eyes were sparkling with enthusiasm and Malory hated knowing that she might have to spoil his plans.

"Earth to Malory." Her father squeezed her hand. "We appear to have lost radio contact."

"Sorry." She smiled. "I was just trying to figure out how to tell you my news."

"Hmm. I find using words usually works," he teased. He leaned forward to brush away a small piece of blossom that had blown into her hair.

"I got a letter today from a place called the Cavendish Foundation," Malory finally began. "They're offering me the chance to train with them this summer and ride the A-Level show circuit." She rushed out the sentence and then braced herself for her dad's reaction.

"So you want to abandon me for the summer, huh?" he said, rubbing his chin.

"No!" Malory exclaimed before realizing he wasn't serious. "Dad!" She aimed a pretend punch at his arm.

Mr O'Neil grinned. "I'm really proud of you, Mal. This sounds like an amazing opportunity."

"It's awesome, Dad," Malory said softly. "You know how much I want to spend time with you this holiday, but this is something that I never dreamed could happen. . . ." Her voice trailed off as she remembered that this was something that might *not* happen if she couldn't get around the issue of horse ownership.

"What aren't you telling me?" Her dad, as ever, was totally tuned in to her emotions.

"Even if I get accepted, I'm not sure I'll be able to go – because I don't own my own horse." Malory felt bad saying the words, knowing how much her dad would love to be able to afford to buy her a pony.

Mr O'Neil didn't say anything for a while. He stared out over the lake as if searching for the answer in the sunlight dancing on the water's surface. "How much do you think it would cost to borrow a horse from your old riding stables?"

Malory's heart swelled with love for her father and how he was always prepared to make whatever sacrifices he could for her. "I'd thought of that, but I'm not sure they would loan out one of their horses."

"What does Ms Carmichael think?" Mr O'Neil asked.

"I haven't asked her about it yet," Malory admitted.

"Then I think that should be our starting point." Mr O'Neil got up and reached down to pull Malory to her feet. "Let's go find her."

"Offer it to him with your hand flat and your thumb tucked in. Don't worry, he won't bite you," Malory encouraged her dad as he held out a horse cookie to Tybalt. They'd stopped by to say hello to the pony on their way to find Ms Carmichael.

Tybalt stretched his neck out and blew through his nostrils.

"I don't think he likes me." Mr O'Neil sounded a little apprehensive. Despite his wife and daughter's love of animals, he wasn't used to being around them.

"That's because he doesn't know you, and he's still wary of strangers," Malory replied. She gave a low whistle. "Come on, Tyb!"

Tybalt's ears pricked forward and, after a pause, he stepped closer and lipped the treat off Mr O'Neil's palm.

"A few months ago he would have been hunched up at the back of the stall, and wouldn't have come to you even if you'd held out a bucket of treats." Ms Carmichael joined them with a salt lick tucked under her arm. She smiled and held out her free hand to shake Mr O'Neil's. "It's good to see you again, Mr O'Neil. We met the day Malory came to try out for her scholarship."

"That's right. You gave me a tour of the stables," said Mr O'Neil. "Thank you so much for everything you've done for Malory this year. Sometimes it seems like the only thing she does here is ride, since that's all she ever talks about. You've made quite an impression on her, Ms Carmichael."

Malory felt her cheeks redden.

Ms Carmichael slid back the bolt on Tybalt's door. "Call me Ali, please. And all I can say is that Malory's been more than we could ever hope for from a scholarship student. Tybalt's living proof of her ability and dedication; in fact, I'd say he owes his place on the yard to her."

"Is that right?" Mr O'Neil raised his eyebrow at his daughter.

"It wasn't just me," she protested, thinking of Amy.

"You must be very proud of Malory," Ms Carmichael added, taking out the old salt block and replacing it with the fresh block. "Especially now that she's been shortlisted for the Cavendish Foundation's programme."

Mr O'Neil nodded. "We're actually here to talk to you about that."

"Great," Ms Carmichael smiled. "How about we go and have a chat in my office?"

They walked down with Ms Carmichael to the lower yard and into the converted stable that was her office. Mr O'Neil looked with interest at the trophies and ribbons in the glass cabinet beneath the window, and Malory wondered if he was imagining a trophy with her name on it taking its place on one of the shelves.

"Why don't we start off with a can of soda to celebrate Mal's offer?" Ms Carmichael suggested. She opened the door of a miniature cooler in the corner of the room.

Mr O'Neil raised his eyebrows at Malory, clearly waiting for her to share her concern with her instructor.

Malory took the can that Ms Carmichael held out. "Thanks." She took a deep breath. "I've been wondering. Can I even compete for the programme? I don't have my own horse and it sounds like everyone who participates will need to have her own."

Malory caught sight of a small muscle jumping in her dad's cheek. Even though he'd known what she'd been about to say, it still couldn't be easy for him to face the fact that he couldn't afford to help out. When Tybalt's future had been uncertain he had felt really sorry that he couldn't swoop in and buy the gelding. The last thing he needed was to be reminded that their lack of money set Malory apart from the other, more privileged girls at school.

"I can see why you're worried about this," Ms Carmichael said thoughtfully. She perched on the edge of her desk. "But I'm sure you can't be the first student the Foundation has approached who doesn't own a pony. Why don't you email them and ask what provisions they make for students in your situation?"

"But if they don't make any provisions and I tell them I don't own a horse, won't that wreck my chance of getting selected?" Malory asked, worried.

"I don't think so. And I would guess that they'll probably be able to point you in the right direction of *where* to get a horse if they can't help you out," Ms Carmichael replied, with a firm nod.

Malory felt her spirits lighten. She glanced across at her dad, who winked at her. "Why don't you do that today?" he offered. He looked back at Ms Carmichael. "I've been told by my daughter that this is some big deal. So if the Cavendish Foundation doesn't help her out, I'll be forced to make like Billy the Kid and head out west to go rope a mustang for her myself."

Malory giggled at her father's terrible fake-Western accent.

"I think you mean Bill Hickok, not Billy the Kid, and I'm not sure a mustang would cut it at the All Schools League Show. But apart from that, I'm sure Malory will appreciate whatever you can do." The corners of Ms Carmichael's mouth twitched playfully.

"I guess a wild horse wouldn't cut it if *that's* the type of animal that will be competing." Mr O'Neil nodded at a picture of Quince on Ali Carmichael's desk.

Ali put down her can. "You can see her in the flesh if you'd like."

Malory followed her dad and Ms Carmichael out of the office, pleased at how well they seemed to be getting along.

In the adjoining loosebox, Quince's lovely grey head was looking out over her door. She whickered gently the moment she saw Ali.

"Do you compete on her?" Mr O'Neil asked.

"Not since I started my job here, although I've kept her training up, and I'm hoping to ride at some of the same shows as Malory this summer." Ms Carmichael smiled.

Malory crossed her fingers behind her back. She felt like it was bad luck to talk about riding the A-Level circuit when she didn't have a horse and still had to get through the final selection process.

"I guess I'd better go email the Foundation now," Malory suggested, waiting for her dad to move to follow her.

But Mr O'Neil seemed content to spend some more time with Quince. "Good idea. I'll wait for you here and see if I can get the hang of offering these horse cookies," he said, fishing one out of his pocket.

As Malory walked over to the Student Centre, she began composing the email in her head. Despite her dad's and Ms Carmichael's optimism, she had a gut feeling that the Cavendish Programme wouldn't be able to help her out with a horse.

Chapter Three

"Hey, Mal, check this out!" Dylan pulled a lavender halter top out of a shopping bag.

"Ooh. Very nice," Malory said enthusiastically. She'd come back to her room after seeing her dad off and was lying on her bed when Dylan burst in to show off her shopping.

"And I got you these since you missed out on coming to town." Dylan rummaged around in the bags she'd dumped on the bed. "Voilà!" She pulled out a pair of dangly silver earrings.

Malory smiled at her friend's sudden penchant for speaking French in homage to Henri. "You didn't have to get me anything," she protested, holding up the earrings to her ears. "But they're adorable. Thanks, Dyl." She leaned forward and hugged her friend.

"No worries. Did you have a good time with your dad?" Dylan cleared a space on the bed so she could sit down.

Malory sat up and hugged her knees. "It was great. We spent some time with your aunt, and she suggested

I contact the Foundation to see if they could find me a horse to ride for the summer."

"That's cool," Dylan enthused. "I just wish I had a horse to loan you." She reached over and brushed a piece of lint off Malory's shoulder. "But I found something out today that will either freak or psych you out." Her eyes sparkled. "Caleb was in town with Josh. Apparently, he's been short-listed for the programme, too!"

Malory ignored the butterfly outbreak in her stomach. She raised her eyebrows at Dylan. "You want to tell me how you found *that* out?"

"I might have accidentally let it slip that *you'?d* gotten a letter from the Cavendish Foundation," Dylan admitted, her mouth tugging up at the corners.

Malory tossed a pillow at her. "You are such a bigmouth, Dylan Walsh!"

"Yeah? Well, this bigmouth also got told by a certain blue-eyed hunk that he's going to be emailing you soon."

Malory's butterflies went crazy. She had thought that if Caleb was in the programme the whole summer would be awkward, but now that she knew he'd had an offer, too, she couldn't help thinking of all the fun they'd shared the summer before. She wondered if she should write to Caleb about not owning a horse when he emailed her. *And how much I'm going to miss Dad if I do get in.*

Whoa! Reality check! What would be the point? Caleb had already made it perfectly clear that he put winning trophies above caring about people. He'd never understand Malory's concern about leaving her dad; he wouldn't be able to see past the fact that the Cavendish offer might well be opening a door to success. And that wasn't what Malory was about, although she was sure she'd never get Caleb to see things from her point of view in a million years.

"Hang on, Mal! You just added sodium hydroxide to the copper sulphate!" Dylan stifled a giggle.

"Huh?" Malory looked at the test tube that she'd just replaced in the rack. For their Monday morning chemistry class they were supposed to add the sodium hydroxide to hydrochloric acid and then note the temperature change. "Are you sure?"

"Sure, she's sure." Lani prodded the blue contents of the test tube with a small spatula. "It's turning to jelly! Do you think if we go ahead and heat the mixture we'll total the lab?"

"What's going on?" Wei Lin called across. They were working on their chemistry experiment in groups of four, and Wei Lin's group was sharing the same table.

"Mal's pulling an absentminded professor on us. Her bod's here but her mind seems to be on the other side of town," Lani said, pretending to grumble.

Malory felt herself go hot. It was true that she was wondering when Caleb would send the email he'd promised, but she was also dwelling on the problems surrounding her summer plans.

"Give her a break – we're all allowed to mess up at

least one experiment," Honey protested. "I think the only person this term who still hasn't is Alex."

Alexandra Cooper looked up from the notebook she'd been using to write up the results of their experiment. "Don't jinx me!"

"No one could jinx you where work is concerned," Dylan teased. "In fact, we're all counting on *you* knowing what the experiment results should be."

Alexandra looked uncertain.

"Relax, she's joking," Malory told her. "It's my fault our experiment is ruined, so I'll take the blame." She looked over to where Ms Marshall was talking with Lynsey's group at the front of the lab. Their teacher wouldn't be favourably impressed with Malory's error. She expected one hundred per cent concentration from her students.

"She was OK when I ran a boiling test tube under cold water last week and it shattered," Honey said, guessing the nature of Malory's thoughts.

"Yeah, I seem to remember that was just after Josh had called to ask you to the end-of-year formal," Dylan chipped in. "What is it about the summer and romance?"

Lani rolled her eyes in mock disgust, making Malory smile.

Dylan's eyes glinted with mischief. "Hey, did I tell you guys that Henri emailed to suggest meeting up this summer? He's spending a couple of weeks of his holiday following the Inca trail and wants to come stay with me for a few days before his trip."

"Did you tell us? Let's see. . ." Lani frowned while drumming her fingers against her chin.

"Only about a hundred times!" Honey and Malory spoke in unison before breaking into laughter.

"You guys, Marshie's looking our way," Wei Lin warned.

They all quickly pretended to be wrapped up in their work; Lani and Dylan looked closely at their test tube while Honey pretended to write in her notebook. Malory let out a sigh of relief when Ms Marshall turned back to the group nearest to her.

"She'll be coming to us next," said Alexandra worriedly as she chewed the end of her pen.

"Listen, why don't you guys share our experiment?" Razina suggested. Wei Lin was firing up the Bunsen burner. "It might spare you some of Marshie's angst."

"Thanks, guys," Malory said gratefully. She helped Alexandra push her pad, pens, and pencils down the table, then glanced at her watch. Ten minutes until their break, then she'd be able to go check her email again. *You can stay focused until then, can't you?* She groaned inwardly. Why was she trying to kid herself? Right now, break-time felt as far away as September!

Even though she'd been waiting for it, Malory felt her stomach do a somersault when she saw that she had a message waiting for her from Caleb.

Hi Mal,
How are things? I saw Dylan in town over the

weekend, and she mentioned that you were short-listed for the Cavendish programme. I bet that she told you I got picked, too. My parents were planning a trip to Europe for the summer, but I'd much rather focus on Cavendish. Nothing comes close to the chance of competing on the A-Level show circuit. All we have to do now is hope like crazy that we get through the final selection. A friend of mine told me that once we've accepted being short-listed we'll have the chance to go to intercollegiate practice sessions. I guess that means we'll be hanging out with each other more than we have lately.

See you at the first practice.

—C

Malory bit her lip. All her excitement at Caleb getting in contact with her slipped away. He assumed she'd be as enthusiastic as he was about being short-listed. *I guess the problems of finding a horse and leaving family behind aren't things he has to worry about. Of course not. Because we're totally different kinds of people.* And he hadn't even mentioned that things were weird between them. It was almost like they'd never dated.

Malory banged out a short reply, determined to keep a detached tone.

Hi Caleb.

It doesn't look like the programme is going to work out for me. But I hope you have a great time this summer.

Best,

Malory

As soon as she hit SEND, her anger began to fizzle out. It wasn't Caleb's fault he had different priorities than her. But suddenly it felt like she was emailing a stranger.

For lunch the girls helped themselves to sandwiches, drinks, and fruit from the cafeteria before heading outside. There was an Adams House meeting planned to brainstorm ideas for the end-of-year party, and everyone had voted to hold a picnic-meeting. The girls had already written suggestions for the event and left them in one of the ballot boxes. Noel Cousins, a senior R.A., was going to announce the most popular choices.

Malory walked with her friends past the library and down to the lawn close to the paddocks. The girls had already begun to form a circle under the trees, and Malory sat cross-legged alongside Razina and Wei Lin.

"Let's cut classes for the rest of the afternoon," Lani suggested, lying back and pillowing her head on her arMs "It's torture making us do maths on a day like this."

"Having riding afterwards makes up for it," Malory pointed out.

"It sure does, and I guess we need all the practice we can get with the All Schools League Show just over a week away," Dylan agreed.

Malory was about to reply when Noel stood up. "What do you say we open the discussion and eat at the same time?" She pushed a stray auburn curl back out of her face and grinned.

"Sounds good to me," Dylan said, digging into her tuna sandwich.

"Since we seniors won't be here next year to keep you all in check," Noel continued, "Rosie is going to try leading things today. So go easy on her!" She dropped a mock curtsy at the round of applause, wolf whistles, and cheers that broke out from the lower school students. The seniors were very popular with their dormmates and they were really going to be missed.

Junior Rosie Williams stood up and flicked her long dark hair over her shoulders. "You're all too kind to welcome me like that," she joked over the last of the applause for the senior class. She unfolded a piece of paper. "Just about everyone has voted for an outdoor movie or a barbecue. There were two other suggestions: an outdoor concert and a staging of our own rodeo with Chuck Braxton as a guest performer."

Dylan raised her eyebrows at Lani. "I wonder who could have dreamed that one up?"

"Guilty as charged." Lani grinned and took a bite out of her apple. Her crush on rodeo star Chuck Braxton was legendary.

"And I think we all know where the concert suggestion came from." Dylan nodded at Faith Holby-Travis on the opposite side of the circle. Faith was an amazing musician, and couldn't quite appreciate that some people had other interests.

"So are we doing a barbecue or an outdoor movie?" Lynsey called out imperiously.

"Let's do both! We could start off with the barbecue

and end the night with a movie. All in favour?" Rosie asked.

All around the picnic hands shot up.

"That makes it easy," said Hayley Cousins, Noel's younger sister. "All we need to do now is decide on what movie we're going to watch, work out the catering, organize decorations, and settle on a date." She listed each item off on her fingers.

"Why doesn't each grade take charge of something?" Noel suggested. "And how about we go for the next to the last Sunday of the term? That's just six days away!"

"OK, so why don't we pick the movie right now before we all take off?" Rosie suggested.

"How about *Legally Blonde*?" Lucy Dowdeswell, the eighth grade student council representative, called out.

"Oh, come on, we must have all seen that at least ten times. Let's have a little imagination!" Elyn Sachs-Cohen replied.

Dylan put down her sandwich. "How about a horror fest? We could all come dressed as our favourite characters and watch back-to-back horror movies."

"It's the wrong time of year," Patience objected coolly. "Save that for Halloween."

"Oh, Dylan never minds being out of sync with seasonal style," Lynsey commented.

"Down, girl," Malory murmured as Dylan opened her mouth to snap back at the girls. "Don't give them the satisfaction."

"Why don't we watch *Charlie's Angels*?" Razina

45

called out. "It's a great girl power movie, and it's totally hilarious."

Several girls nodded, laughing.

"What about a dress code?" Patience asked. "Less than a week is a pretty short time to organize an outfit."

Malory swapped glances with Dylan. Patience's father was Edward Duvall, the famous author. With his wealth and connections, Patience could ask for a Yoshiharu Ito designer jacket and it would be couriered to her by next-day air.

"We're already dressing up for the Saint Kits formal," Lani argued. "I vote we dress down for this one --something in line with a night of chilling out."

"Sounds good to me," Hayley agreed as she tossed a peach to her sister.

"Let's have a beach theme then," Razina suggested. "We could try to get permission to use the pool for the first part of the night before we barbecue and watch the movie."

"All in favor?" said Rosie.

All of the girls raised their hands with enthusiasm.

"Wow, that's gotta be the easiest planning of a dorm party yet." Rosie grinned. "Kind of makes you feel unnecessary, huh?" She winked at Noel who was lying on her stomach taking a bite out of the peach Hayley had thrown her.

"Don't forget, we taught you everything you know," the senior replied breezily.

"It's going to be pretty weird not having the seniors here next year," Dylan murmured.

Malory nodded. She was still trying to adjust to the fact that they'd been at Chestnut Hill for nearly an entire year. When they came back after the summer break, they would be eighth-graders! She just wished she knew for sure what her own plans would be during the holiday. So much depended on what the Foundation said about borrowing a horse. *Once I get that worked out, I can start dealing with the idea of leaving Dad for the holiday.*

By the time their riding lesson came along, Malory couldn't wait to get into the saddle. Even though the All Schools League Show was still two weeks away, anxiety was beginning to kick in and she hoped that sailing over a course of jumps on Tybalt would help her to relax.

She pulled a stalk of hay out of Tybalt's mouth as she led him onto the yard. "Did you sneak one last mouthful?" she asked playfully.

Tybalt gave her a friendly nudge and then blew out as she went to check the girth, making it impossible to cinch it properly. "You don't want the saddle to slip, do you?" she told him. The moment Tybalt took a breath Malory was ready to pull the girth up another hole. "All done," she said as she lowered the saddle flap.

Out of the corner of her eye, Malory could see Lynsey buckling up her chinstrap. Bluegrass, Lynsey's pony, swished his tail at a pesky fly, but apart from that he looked his usual calm self. *He's definitely over his blip.* Blue had gone through a minor crisis of boredom a few weeks back, and Malory had been amazed when Lynsey had sought her out, and then had *taken* her advice on how to unwind the pony. Not that it had fostered any sort of a friendship between them. *Lynsey wouldn't be caught dead fraternizing with the scholarship girl whose dad owns a shoe store.*

Malory rode past Lynsey and in through the riding arena's main doors. She knew she had plenty of friends at Chestnut Hill who appreciated her for who she was, and weren't bothered by her lack of wealth or connections.

Most of the class was already riding around the ring to warm up the ponies. As Malory began to trot around the arena she glanced across at the jumps that had been set out. The yellow-and-black spread cross pole looked like the trickiest fence on the course. She'd need to ride with plenty of speed as well as a clear line of approach. Suddenly Tybalt's quarters swung out and Malory used her outside leg behind the girth to get him back on the track. The gelding had picked up the pace without her noticing and was crowding Colourado, who had been trotting a little ahead of them in the ring.

"Sorry," Mal apologized to Lani, who had glanced over her shoulder. She made sure that she kept her focus for the rest of the warm-up until Ms Carmichael waved them into a group in the centre.

Tybalt began playing with his bit and shifting restlessly. Malory tried to make herself relax in the saddle, sitting deep with her legs barely touching his sides. She wondered if the other junior team riders were feeling the pressure of the looming competition.

They hadn't won any of the interschool competitions that year and Malory was longing to prove what a great instructor Ali Carmichael was. She still found it hard to believe that some of the students had signed a petition to have Ali replaced earlier that year. There was no getting away from the fact that Allbrights was more successful than Chestnut Hill in the league stakes, but Malory had total faith in Ms Carmichael. *And the best way of proving that she's every bit as good an instructor as Elizabeth Mitchell is to win the All Schools League Show.*

Malory leaned forward and smoothed Tybalt's neck. She knew that the gelding also had a lot to prove. Coming home with a red ribbon from the show would go a long way to silencing his critics – like Lynsey Harrison.

"I want to do something a little different today," Ms Carmichael announced. "I'd like you to all watch one another's performance, because I'll be asking you to comment on each other's strengths and weaknesses. It's one thing to be able to feel what you've done wrong on a round and quite another to be able to see what faults another rider is making."

Malory caught sight of Dylan's grimace and knew that she was anticipating Lynsey's comments on Morello's performance. Even if the paint pony outjumped every other horse in the class, Lynsey would still find something disparaging to say. As far as she was concerned, unless a pony had an A-1 pedigree, it had no right to share a space with *her* magnificent horse.

"Lynsey, you can ride first," Ms Carmichael said.

When Lynsey trotted Bluegrass past Tybalt, she rode exaggeratedly wide. "Tybalt seems like he's in a mood today – I don't want him attacking Blue," she called.

"Face it, Mal. She's never going to forgive Tyb for throwing her off in front of the whole class last year," Dylan muttered as Malory gritted her teeth in anger.

Malory watched as Lynsey got Bluegrass settled into a steady canter to approach the first jump. Bluegrass made clearing the fence look easy as he popped over it and cantered over to the wall. Lynsey held the pony back to the last stride before urging him over, and her face registered annoyance as Bluegrass clipped the top row of bricks with his forelegs. *She's holding him back too much*, Malory thought. They cleared the rest of the course, but Lynsey still looked unhappy when they came back to the group.

"Well done, Lynsey," Ms Carmichael said. "I'm going to throw this out to the class. Can anyone critique Lynsey's performance?"

"I thought she rode really well and it was just bad luck on the wall," Paris Mackenzie piped up.

"Anyone else?" Ms Carmichael prompted. "Malory?"

Malory hesitated. "I think that maybe Lynsey sidelined Bluegrass a little, which is why she got the knockdown."

"Interesting theory," Ms Carmichael said. "Can you expand on it a bit more?"

Malory swallowed. "Lynsey was taking more control than usual. Usually she and Bluegrass are totally in tune with each other. Lynsey took a bigger percentage of control this time and I think it unsettled Bluegrass."

Malory could feel Lynsey's eyes on her. Of course the snotty girl wouldn't take kindly to having her riding criticized. *Oh, well. She'll get her turn to comment on me soon enough.*

Dylan went next and would have turned in a good round, except Morello brought down the triple bar. It didn't help that it was the first jump out of a corner that Dylan was never great at.

"Comments?" Ms Carmichael invited.

"Dylan forgot to give Morello his special pills," Lynsey remarked in a low voice.

Ms Carmichael raised her eyebrows – she had obviously heard. "Anyone else?" she asked sharply.

"Dylan dropped the impulsion on the approach. She let Morello sort himself out and he wasn't in a good rhythm in the last three strides before takeoff," Honey volunteered.

"Would you agree, Dylan?" said Ms Carmichael.

Dylan nodded as she smoothed Morello's damp neck. "Totally. I was so concerned about getting him on to the right leg coming out of the corner that I forgot about the fence until it was too late."

"It's just a good thing the reserve doesn't get to ride at the All Schools League Show. The odds are stacked against us enough as it is," Lynsey complained with a pointed look at Tybalt.

Ms Carmichael ignored Lynsey and waved at Malory to go next.

Tybalt began fighting against the reins from the get-go,

so Malory cantered him in a large circle until he began to accept her hands. His stride was springy when he approached the first jump and she half-halted him to remind him that they were going to tackle the course as a team. Tybalt responded by making a large but controlled jump over the first fence. As soon as they landed, Malory worked to keep him to the same controlled pace. For a moment she was aware that her performance was being watched critically by the rest of the class and wondered if anyone would pick up on the fact that Tybalt was trying to fight her a little. *Concentrate on the next fence*, she told herself as they turned to the spread. If she was this aware of her classmates watching, how would she feel if she ever got in front of the Cavendish judges?

Tybalt hesitated as they approached the yellow-and-black spread. Malory could see that the front pole was higher on the left and the back pole on the right, so she took her line a little to the right of centre, making the jump an ascending spread. To her relief, Tybalt jumped large, but retained the gorgeous outline that he'd produced for the first jump.

The moment they landed, Malory shifted her weight to the right and put pressure on with her leg behind the girth so that Tybalt switched his lead. "Good boy," she praised as they cantered along to the wall.

Although Tybalt went clear, Malory felt exhausted rather than elated when they cantered back to the group. It had been a tough call holding the gelding in check while asking for maximum drive to tackle the fences.

"Well done, Malory," Ms Carmichael congratulated her. She turned to the group. "Comments?"

"Tybalt seemed a little distracted. I got the impression he wasn't totally settled," Honey said softly. "But that makes it even more of a great job that he went clear."

Malory agreed that Tybalt *had* been distracted. They had hardly offered the polished act the Cavendish Foundation would be looking for. She doubted that the ability to handle difficult ponies was a priority for the programme. The other riders would probably have their own polished pedigree ponies who wouldn't be fazed by the pressure of top flight showing.

In the end, like it always seemed to, everything came down to having a privileged background. *Even if I do get offered a horse, I can't possibly have enough competitive experience to get through the final selection.*

Malory cross-tied Tybalt in the barn and took her time sponging him down. She squeezed water over his glossy dark coat before following over it with a sweat scraper. "There, I bet you're feeling a lot cooler now," she told him as she buckled on his anti-sweat rug.

"So, that was some kind of fluke, huh?" Lynsey stopped just outside Tybalt's stall on her way to the tack room. She pulled her blonde hair out of the net she used when riding and shook it back over her shoulders.

Malory frowned. "What?"

"That clear round. He's just not first-class material – when are you going to face that?"

Malory swallowed hard. Lynsey knew exactly what to say to get to her.

Dylan had walked up in time to hear Lynsey's criticism. "Don't you ever let up on Tybalt?" she asked sharply. "I bet deep down you know that Malory and Tybalt are serious competition for the Cavendish programme final selection. And it would totally kill you if Mal got accepted and you didn't!"

"As if I would really worry about going up against someone who's never even ridden in an A-Level show!" Lynsey retorted.

Dylan spun around to confront Lynsey but Malory beat her to it. "You know something? I don't care if I never get to ride in an A-Level show if it means that I end up obsessing about being the best. If *you're* the kind of person that the Cavendish Riding Programme is looking for, then I'm glad that my application form is still sitting on my desk!"

Lynsey's jaw was as good as on the floor as Malory pushed past, pausing long enough to snatch Tybalt's saddle and bridle off the wall before storming down the aisle.

"Mal, wait up!" Dylan called from behind as Malory stalked into the tack room. "Wow, your temper meltdowns are well worth waiting for. That was truly awesome! I never thought I'd be turning to Malory O'Neil for lessons on how to put Lynsey in her place."

"Don't." Malory shook her head. She was already

wishing she hadn't lost it in front of Lynsey. "I think I'm going to stay for a while and clean Tybalt's tack." She wished Dylan would pick up on her hint: *I want to be alone.*

Dylan hovered uncertainly in the doorway. "Do you want a hand? You don't want to be late for study hall."

"I'll be OK, I promise," Malory replied, appreciating her friend's concern.

Dylan gave her an empathetic smile before turning to go.

Once Dylan had left, Malory took a deep breath, inhaling the smell of leather and saddle soap. Lavender oil worked to relax Tybalt, but the tack room always did it for her.

"Hey, Malory."

She turned around to see Alessandra di Schiapari, another Adams House student and the co-captain of the Senior Riding Team, walk into the room. She was carrying Quest's saddle. "I thought I'd clean it up here. It's a lot cooler than down on the main block," she explained.

Malory nodded. Alessandra gave Quest's tack a thorough going-over every time she rode the dappled grey gelding. She was a perfectionist in every aspect of her riding, which explained why she was such a key member of the senior team. "I heard you got short-listed for the Cavendish Riding Programme."

Malory smiled ruefully. "News travels fast around here." She paused. "I know it's a really great offer, but I'm having trouble getting my head around it."

Alessandra nodded. "It's a big deal – being away from home all year and then again for the summer. And I guess the prospect of competing at the A-Level shows brings its own pressure, too?"

"Tell me about it," Malory agreed.

"I only know because I was selected for the same programme," Alessandra confessed.

"Really?" Malory exclaimed, although she knew she shouldn't be surprised. Alessandra was one of the most talented riders in the school. Malory watched the senior put Quest's bridle on a blanket box and reach down for a tray of cleaning materials.

Alessandra nodded. "Right up until the last minute I wasn't going to send in my acceptance form. It was my brother's last summer at home before he took a job in London, and I wanted to spend time with him before he left."

"What made you change your mind?" Malory was curious.

"Liz Mitchell persuaded me that it was a huge opportunity and if I threw it away I might end up really regretting it." She began to unbuckle Quest's bridle to get it ready to wash. "She was right. It wasn't just training with some awesome instructors and the chance to ride the A-Level circuit. It was also the bond it helped build between Quest and me."

Malory appreciated how open the senior was being with her. "I emailed the Foundation to see if they could loan me a horse. I'm not sure they'll accept me without one, but you're right, it is an incredible opportunity."

"The summer camp is hard work but by the end of it I bet you'll be saying the blood, sweat, and tears were all worth it." Alessandra smiled. "I'll keep my fingers crossed that you can find a horse."

Malory ran down the corridor towards study hall. She was already five minutes late. "Relax," Dylan called out from her seat near the window as Malory hurried into the room. "Brighty's going to be late." She nodded to the white board at the front of the room. Ms Bright had written that she was going to be ten minutes late and they were to get started on their work. Malory heaved a sigh of relief. Whenever their social studies teacher was supervising study hall she took her duties as seriously as when they were in class. Ms Bright wouldn't have gone easy on her for being late.

Malory dropped her bag on her desk and then went over to Dylan's desk. "I wanted to stop by the student centre to see if the Foundation had emailed me. I started talking to Alessandra in the tack room, though, so I ran out of time."

"You could always use Dyl's BlackBerry," Lani said, turning around from her desk in front. She waved Honey over from a seat across the aisle. Honey came over and took a seat on Dylan's desk, right on top of her math book.

Dylan reached around to her bag on the back of her chair and pulled out her handy little BlackBerry. She carefully passed it to Malory.

"They might not have had time to reply yet," Malory

mumbled as she typed on the small keys.

"Well? Anything?" Dylan demanded when Malory's account flicked up on the screen.

"One message." Malory nodded, feeling more queasy than excited. Her friends all held their breath as she opened the email. Malory read it twice to make sure she'd got their reply straight. She looked up at her friends, a blank expression on her face.

"Well?" Dylan prompted again.

Malory swallowed. "They said no." She felt like someone had just dumped a bucket of ice water over her. "They don't accept applicants without horses."

Chapter Four

Malory unbuckled Tybalt's head collar. "Go!"

The gelding sprang away from her and galloped across to the chestnut tree in the middle of the paddock. He ignored the other horses, who had stopped grazing to watch him. Tybalt pawed at the ground and turned around before sinking onto his knees. Malory leaned against the gate to watch him roll, first on one side and then the other. Finally, Tybalt scrambled to his feet and shook the dust off. Malory's fingers itched to run over with a body brush and bring a glossy sheen back to his coat.

As she watched the dark gelding, her thoughts strayed back to the email she'd received from the Foundation. It was pretty much all she'd been thinking about over the last two days. *I shouldn't be so disappointed since this means I get to spend the summer with Dad.* She kicked at a small pebble. No matter how much she tried to convince herself that not going ahead with the programme was for the best, it was hard not to dwell on everything she'd be missing out on.

"Tybalt's enjoying himself." Honey's voice broke through Malory's thoughts. She was leading Moonlight Minuet down the path.

"Let me get that." Malory unhooked the clasp on the gate and pushed it open.

"Thanks." Honey unbuckled the halter and stood back as the grey mare trotted over to the other horses. When Minnie lay down to roll, Nutmeg, a cute buckskin pony, stopped grazing and walked over to say hello to her.

"I don't how Nutmeg manages to get that close without getting caught by Min's hooves," Honey commented as Minnie rolled right over with her legs stretched out.

"Mmm." Malory was only partly concentrating. After a few minutes went by, she noticed that Honey had grown quiet and was staring over the distant fields. "Honey, are you OK?"

Honey didn't answer right away. She scuffed the turf with her heel. "I'm waiting for a call about Sam," she admitted.

Malory felt a spasm of anxiety. Honey's twin brother had leukemia and for the last six months had been receiving treatment at the medical centre in Cheney Falls. *Please don't let it be bad news*, Malory hoped as she twisted Tybalt's lead rope around her hand.

"I've been so scared that he won't be able to fight the cancer off." Honey's voice was barely above a whisper.

"Why didn't you tell me you've been worried?" Mal

hugged her friend, but she already knew the ans-wer. Honey was very similar to her when it came to bottling things up and locking them away. Malory felt frustrated with herself. She should have figured out that Honey was worrying about Sam. *And here I am stressing about some riding programme.*

"Even though Sam seems to have pulled through this time, we won't know if he's beaten the cancer for sure until we get the results of the blood tests," Honey confessed. "He's meeting with his consultant this afternoon. I thought that they would have phoned by now. It's getting pretty late."

"Have you checked to see if you're getting a signal?" Malory asked. "I know that there are some places on campus where it doesn't come through."

Honey slipped her mobile phone out of her jeans pocket and stared at the screen. "Sheesh! My battery's dead." She looked back up. "I'm going back up to the house to recharge it." She held out Minnie's head collar and lead rope. "Could you take these back to the barn?"

"Sure. Good luck," Malory called as her friend raced up the path. She wanted to tell Honey that everything would be all right but she'd learned from bitter experience that sometimes, no matter how much you longed for someone to get better, it didn't happen.

Malory sighed and hooked the head collars over her arm. She secured the gate and then walked back up to the barn. Tybalt and Minnie had been the last two ponies to be turned out, which meant that every stall was empty with its door wide open. A portable radio was standing on an upturned bucket, and Kelly and Sarah were singing along while they mucked out the stables.

"Do you want a hand?" Malory offered.

"We're almost done, thanks." Kelly broke off from singing into the broom handle like it was a microphone.

"Well, *I'm* almost done, anyway. Kelly's too busy practising for her *American Idol* audition to be much use," Sarah teased.

Malory chuckled as she went to hang Minnie's head collar on the hook outside her stall.

Ms Carmichael walked into the barn carrying two buckets full of vegetable peelings. "I just paid the kitchen a visit," she explained, putting them down. She wiped her palms on her trousers. "I'm glad you're here, Malory. I was going to send a message for you to come down to see me."

"Is everything OK?" Malory asked in surprise.

"I wanted to talk to you about your application for the Cavendish Programme. I know how disappointed you were when they said they couldn't loan you a horse." Ms Carmichael got straight to the point.

Malory nodded. She'd told Ali the news the day before, and her instructor had been full of sympathy and disappointment for her.

"So I went to see Dr Starling today," Ms Carmichael continued.

Malory frowned. What did the principal have to do with this?

"I explained how important I feel it is that you

attend the programme if you get through the final selection." Ali Carmichael paused. "The long and short of it is that she's given permission for you to borrow one of the school's horses. So you can send in your acceptance form after all."

I can borrow one of the school's horses! Malory heard the words dancing around her head as happiness bloomed inside her. It was like Christmas and her birthday all at once! *But which horse?* She didn't dare to hope she'd be allowed to take Tybalt. Ms Carmichael would be sure to think it would be too much pressure for him.

"You're welcome to choose any of the riding school ponies, although I suspect a certain dark brown gelding's details will be accompanying yours." Ms Carmichael smiled, dispelling Malory's doubts.

Malory stared at her instructor. "Really?" was all she managed to say.

Ms Carmichael nodded. "You've more than earned it, Malory. I wouldn't trust our four-legged friends to every student." Her smile stretched even farther. "But I won't hold you up any longer. I'm sure you're dying to go share the news with your friends. You need to let the Foundation know right away, though; the first training session is just four days away on Sunday at Allbrights."

The same day as our dorm party! "Thank you," Malory said, her voice high with excitement. "Thank you, Ms Carmichael. This is just great. . . . I mean . . . thank you."

"Go!" Ms Carmichael said, shooing Malory away

with her hands. "Come back when you've got a grip on your vocabulary."

Malory laughed and sprinted up the aisle. The summer stretched in front of her, full of possibilities. She was able to apply for the programme, and Tybalt would be coming with her!

Malory raced past the outdoor arenas and took the path up to Adams She could see Dylan, Lani, and Honey heading over the lawn towards her. Malory slowed her pace as she realized that Honey would have found out about Sam by now. Her own news was nothing compared with what was going on in Honey's life.

"What's the news on Sam?" she demanded the moment she met up with her friends.

"It's all good," Honey said with a wide smile.

"In fact, it's fabulous," Dylan told her.

"I'd say it's a definite fabulous overload," Lani put in.

"If fabulous was ice cream we'd be buried in the stuff and trying to eat our way free." Dylan grinned.

"Enough already," Malory protested. "Will somebody tell me what the deal is?"

"All of Sam's blood tests came back clear." Honey's eyes shone. "He's in remission!"

"That's. . ." Malory sought for the right word.

"Fabulous?" Dylan supplied with a grin.

"Totally!" Malory threw her arms around Honey.

"See, we told you," Dylan teased.

Honey gently extricated herself from Malory's hug.

"My parents are going to drive over this weekend with Sam. They want us to all have a picnic together on Saturday to celebrate. They know how great you guys have been."

Malory thought back to Christmas time, when Honey had been so worried about her twin that she had broken school rules and gone to see him in the hospital without permission. "That would be great. I'd really like to meet your family."

"You were in some hurry when we first saw you, Mal," Lani commented as they sat down on one of the benches that lined the path. "We expected to see some two-headed monster in hot pursuit."

"Oh, Lani – don't talk about Lynsey like that," Dylan chided.

Malory smiled. "You know you talked about fabulous being an ice cream? Well, I've got the hot fudge sauce to go on top," she told her friends. "Ms Carmichael arranged for me to borrow Tybalt for the summer. I can send off my acceptance forms for the short list!"

Dylan fanned her face with her hands. "Uh-oh. I don't think I can take much more good news."

Honey squeezed Malory's arm. "You and Tybalt will be covered in red ribbons by the end of the summer!"

"I haven't thought that far ahead yet," Malory admitted. "I've still got to get through the final selection. It's going to be hard work getting a good performance out of Tybalt at the All Schools League Show next week."

"You've got about as much chance of messing up at the show as we do of being buried alive in ice cream," Dylan said.

Malory felt a warm tingling inside. Her friends' confidence in her meant a great deal. At the start of the year she'd felt completely alone when it came to tackling new challenges. Now she had her own mini cheerleading squad!

"I wonder if good news comes in threes, like bad news is supposed to," Lani mused.

"If it does, then maybe Dr Starling will announce that it's way too hot to expect any of us to study and she's canceling classes for the rest of term," Honey suggested.

"Or Lynsey will come down with a major throat infection and lose her voice until summer holiday," Dylan jumped in.

Malory laughed. She didn't care if there was no more good news for the rest of the year. Right now she had more than enough to celebrate!

Later that evening, Malory called her dad to tell him that she was emailing in her acceptance forMs "Are you sure you don't mind changing our plans for the summer?" she checked.

"We're still going horseback riding and we're still going to have those barbecues – we're just going to move them to the *next* holiday," her dad assured her.

"Hot dogs for Thanksgiving?" Malory joked.

"Hey, just because something's a compromise

doesn't mean we can't make it work. I'm so proud of you, sweetheart. I might even get a photo of you jumping Tybalt and blow it up into a poster. I'll be able to put it up in the store and tell all my customers you're the next Debbie Macbeth."

"I think you mean Debbie McDonald," Malory said in amusement. "Unless Debbie Macbeth is an Olympic rider who quotes Shakespeare! Are you serious about coming to watch me in some of the shows if I manage to get into the programme?"

"Are you kidding? The thought of that poster's put me in a creative mood. I'm going to start making my pom-poms tonight. I might even go the whole way and design a Team Malory T-shirt."

Malory laughed. Her dad was usually shy and never did stuff that drew attention to himself, so the idea of him waving pom-poms in the air was pretty wild.

"Listen, I've always found that there are times when things are just meant to be," he went on more seriously. "I think this is one of those times. So you've got to go for it, and don't think for one moment that you won't get through that final selection, OK? You're an O'Neil, and that means you're already a winner."

Malory felt a burst of pride. The Harrisons didn't have the patent on being proud of their achievements after all. "I won't forget it, Dad," she told him, equally serious. "I'll do my best to make you proud, I promise."

"They're here!" Honey jumped off the steps outside Adams and ran down the driveway towards the blue

SUV that was pulling into a parking space.

"I guess we should give them a moment," Lani murmured to the other girls.

Malory and Dylan nodded as the back passenger door opened before the engine even stopped. A tall boy wearing a red baseball cap threw his arms around Honey and then mussed up her hair. Honey shouted with laughter and knocked his cap to the ground.

"I guess we ought to get over there before it turns nasty," Dylan joked. At the same time, Mr and Mrs Harper climbed out of the car and waved them over.

"Mal, Dylan, this is my brother, Sam," Honey introduced them as they gathered. She sounded out of breath. "You've already met Lani."

Sam winked. "Under fairly interesting circumstances." He was referring to the time Lani turned up at the hospital where he was getting treatment. She had helped get Honey there when they should have been watching an interschool riding competition. "You've become a legend among my friends back home," Sam added. "They all want an e-photo of the girl who planned the mission to help Honey go AWOL."

"They can't have one. I wouldn't want to be responsible for the mass rush across the Atlantic to meet me in the flesh once they'd seen it," Lani replied, straight-faced.

"In your dreams, Hernandez. You'd need *me* in the frame for that to happen," Dylan quipped.

Even though Sam's blue eyes glinted at the banter, Malory could still see the telltale signs that he'd been through a major illness. He had bags under his eyes and lines of tiredness around his mouth. She could also see that he'd lost a lot of weight compared to photos of him in Honey's album.

"I hate to break up the party, but I could use a hand with this," Mr Harper called. He was trying to wrestle an enormous wicker basket from the trunk. "Did you leave *any* items on the supermarket shelves?" he asked Honey's mother.

"You know Mum's on a campaign to fatten me up," Sam said, going to rescue his dad.

"I think we might have to eat in the parking lot," Mr Harper groaned as they heaved the picnic basket out.

"No way! We've found the perfect spot," Honey said.

"Let me guess, down by the lake," Mrs Harper said, tucking a strand of blonde hair behind her ear. "Wonderful."

"Not by the lake," Honey told her. "It's even more wonderful than that. In fact, it's just about our favourite place on campus, right girls?"

"Right," Malory chorused with the others.

Mrs Harper looked mystified. "Lead the way," she said. "It must be really special."

"Well, it definitely is different," Sam said as he and Mr Harper set down the picnic basket.

"Isn't it just?" Honey ignored her twin's sarcastic tone.

Malory agreed with Honey. Sitting under the leafy

canopy of a maple tree and looking out at the brand-new cross-country course was the perfect picnic place, in her opinion.

"We figure Ms Carmichael will extend the cross-country module now that we have our own setup," Honey told her family.

Sam groaned. "Is there any chance that we might get by without talking about horses for the next few hours?"

"None whatsoever," Honey said sweetly.

"So horses aren't your thing?" Lani asked Sam.

"Nope, give me a ball sport any day." Sam leaned back and propped his head on his arMs "I played rugby back home."

"Ever been to a baseball game?" Lani asked with a grin.

"I was planning to, but I've been sort of busy since we arrived here," Sam said. "I'm guessing that it would be a little more fun than hanging out at the Cheney Falls Medical Centre?"

"It's a tough call, but you do get to go home with all your own hair," Lani teased boldly.

Malory bit her lip, afraid that Sam was sensitive about being bald, but Lani had obviously pitched her humour just right.

Sam laughed. "That decides it. I'd definitely be up for seeing a game someday soon."

Mrs Harper shook out the tartan rug and began setting out plates. "What is that jump over there?" She pointed at two thick wooden poles that were close to each other at one end but wide apart at the other. From where they were sitting at the side, it looked like a giant V.

"That's a corner jump," Malory told her. "It has to be taken at the narrowest end."

"It looks pretty dangerous. How do the horses know which side of it to jump so they don't get stuck in the middle?" Honey's mom popped the lid of a container of cold chicken drumsticks, and the smell of barbecue sauce made Malory's mouth water.

"That's up to the rider," Lani replied. "Although we can't wait to see Dylan attempt it on Morello. He's as argumentative as she is." She winked at Dylan. "Maybe you should actually ride at the widest part so he'll jump the narrowest."

"Ah, reverse psychology," Malory nodded, playing along.

"Personally, I can't wait to see Colourado's reaction to the course," Dylan responded. "He'll probably be going so fast he won't even notice the jumps!" She tossed a peanut in the air and neatly caught it in her mouth. "Maybe we can get Mal to send out the right vibes to slow him down."

"Oh, yes. I hear you're the horse whisperer of Chestnut Hill," Mr Harper said to Malory as he bit into a celery stick dipped in hummus. His blue eyes were full of interest.

"I wouldn't say that," Malory said, embarrassed.

"Oh, no? Who is it that's been offered a place on the prestigious Cavendish Riding Programme?" Honey chipped in.

"What's that?" Mrs Harper asked.

"It's a training programme for the best of the best," Dylan said teasingly but with a hint of pride in her voice.

"That's absolutely wonderful, Malory. Your father must be thrilled," Mrs Harper enthused. She passed around a box of cookies.

"Thanks, but I haven't made the final selection yet," Malory said, her cheeks burning.

"You will," Lani said confidently. "Wow, are these real cucumber sandwiches?" She picked up one of the thin bread triangles. "I thought these things only existed in stories. You guys actually eat these?"

"Try one, you'll be surprised at how good they are," Mrs Harper urged.

"Although it does help if you like cucumber," Sam said when Lani took a bite and clearly didn't like what she discovered.

"I take it cucumber sandwiches aren't going to rate highly on your list of favourite foods?" Mrs Harper smiled.

"I'd call it a definite experience of the palate!" Lani was apologetic for not being able to finish her sandwich. "But it was worth it just so I can say I've been on a real English picnic."

"I've always said cucumber tasted like watered-down slugs," Sam remarked.

"And how would you know what slugs taste like?" Lani challenged, her eyes sparkling.

"Hey, we weren't always this classy," Sam replied,

waving his hand over the picnic blanket. "There was a time when Mum went through an organic phase and the only food she'd put on the table was what she could find in the garden. On our first-ever holiday in France we were really disappointed to find escargots on the menu – we'd been hoping for something out of the ordinary."

Honey crumpled up some of the discarded aluminum foil and threw it at Sam. "You are such a liar!"

Sam tossed the wrapper back and hit Lani on the shoulder instead. She immediately flicked a roasted peanut back at him. Malory ducked as Sam threw a chip back at Lani. *If you can't beat them, join them,* she thought, flicking a small piece of cold chicken that hit Sam on his cheek. Malory giggled when she saw the splotch of mayonnaise it left behind.

"I believe 'time out,' is the expression I want" Mr Harper said hastily as Sam picked up a slice of quiche.

"Yes, let's call it a draw. I even have prizes," Mrs Harper agreed. She rummaged in her oversized purse and pulled out four silver gift bags. "They're Ruby & Millie. I asked my mother to send them over from London because I thought you might enjoy experimenting with some new cosmetics for the formal."

Sam held his hands up. "I think I'll pass and allow the girls the victory."

"Are you sure? I think you'd look real cute in a number three, Burnished Bronze," Lani teased, gesturing at him with a lipstick.

Malory smiled at their antics as Sam pretended to grab the lipstick from Lani and apply it to his lips. It was clear that these two were crazy about each other, even if neither of them would admit it. *I wish Caleb and I could be so relaxed together.* Although, when she thought back to their relationship, she had to admit that they had gone through a short period where they had just had fun in each other's company. But it had been all too soon before they'd hit the strain of their differing priorities. Why couldn't things be simple for her like they seemed for Honey, or lighthearted like they were for Lani? Even Dylan's long-distance romance seemed preferable to her own failed relationship.

"This is fantastic, thanks so much, Mrs Harper," Malory said, bringing her attention back to the picnic. The makeup wouldn't just come in handy for the formal in a week's time. It would also be great for the dorm party tomorrow night. Her bag had foundation, blush, eye shadow, mascara, and lipstick. *If only I had someone to admire the final result.*

As if on cue, Lani said, "I bet the Saint Kits boys will be fighting each other to dance with us."

"Not me – I'm going to get Henri to come over and take me to the formal," Dylan announced.

Malory stared at her friend. Even though there was clearly no chance of Henri flying from France for the formal, she couldn't help wondering why she couldn't be that confident with boys. A giggle rose up inside her at the thought of marching up to Caleb, hitting him over the head with a club, and dragging him off to the dance, cavewoman style.

Dylan leaned closer to Malory and dropped her voice. "Has Caleb been in touch with you about the formal?"

Malory bit her lip. "No. Things are still really awkward between us."

"Hey, formal or no formal, you have to find out what's going on with him. If you both get accepted into the programme, it could make for an awkward summer – with a capital A." Dylan sounded concerned.

"I know," Malory admitted. "But it's easier just letting things go." She was all too aware of how different her approach to boys was from her friends'.

"Well, it's your first training session tomorrow. You'll have to talk to him then," Dylan reminded her.

Malory nodded. If it weren't for the fact that she would have to face Caleb, she'd be really looking forward to tomorrow. As it was, nerves were starting to take over whenever she thought of coming face-to-face with him again

Why does he have this effect on me? Is it because I still like him? A lot?

Chapter Five

Malory couldn't decide if she wanted the next two hours to fly or crawl by. It was eleven o'clock, and at one she would be leaving for Allbrights and her first intercollegiate training session. She pushed a piece of melon around her bowl as she wondered if Caleb was this worried about seeing her. *Probably not. It's pretty obvious that he's hardly thought of me at all lately.*

"You've been staring down at that bowl of fruit salad for a whole five minutes. Are you waiting for it to give you permission to eat it?"

Malory looked up at Lani, who was sitting opposite her. "You know how I get when I'm nervous."

"Here, I have an idea." Dylan leaned across with her fork and began pushing at the fruit. She quickly arranged the cherries into eyes, the chopped banana into a nose, and part of a pineapple ring into an upward-turned mouth. The rest of the fruit was left to form a crazy hairstyle. "There, it's smiling at you. It wants to be eaten."

"You're crazy, Dylan! I'm not in kindergarten!" But

Malory couldn't help grinning. She made herself pop a piece of pineapple into her mouth. She looked over at Eleanor Dixon, the captain of the junior jumping team, who had also been short-listed for the Cavendish Programme. She was scarfing down her scrambled eggs without any sign of nerves.

"Something tells me it's not just the riding that's got you edgy," Lani said. "It's because Caleb's going to be there, isn't it?"

Malory shrugged. "We won't have to spend any time together. We'll be too busy focusing on the class."

"Hmm." Lani didn't look convinced.

"Do you have any idea what you're going to be doing during the session?" Honey asked.

"Nope." Malory was relieved to change the subject.

There was no point talking about Caleb. Nothing had changed; he still had that intense competitive streak, and she wanted no part of it. *He'll never understand that I'm not concerned about coming home with red ribbons, but that I just want to take the chance for Tybalt and me to improve together.* And yet she couldn't shake the feeling that she and Caleb had unfinished business. "I know that this first training session is being taught by Allbrights's Chief of Riding," she told her friends.

"Elizabeth Mitchell? Now *that* will make Lynsey happy," Dylan said dryly. It was common knowledge that Lynsey, along with many Chestnut Hill riding students, held Allbrights's chief instructor in high esteem.

"It will give her a chance to see that Ms Carmichael is every bit as good as Ms Mitchell," Honey commented.

"I think she'll be too busy keeping an eye on Tybalt to do any comparing of instructors," Malory said. Lynsey had already made several cutting remarks about the fact that Malory was training on the brown gelding.

"I think after you chewed her up and spat her out when she said you and Tybalt weren't ready for the A-Level circuit that she'll be keeping any other comments to herself," Dylan said.

"To be fair, she had a point, even if I didn't appreciate the way she put it," Malory said. "I know that Tybalt has got amazing potential but I'm not sure that he's ready to produce it for the top shows this summer. And I don't have any major show-ring experience."

"Why should it bother her? You'll be in the programme as individuals, not team members," Lani pointed out.

"I think she sees any performance that I turn in as a reflection on the school, which includes her." Malory gnawed her thumbnail. Was she right to be putting Tybalt under this level of pressure? He'd been doing so well lately. The last thing she wanted was to undo all of the hard work she'd put in.

"If you ask me, Lynsey will be too busy worrying about whether she should wear her Sauvage or her Chio bikini to the dorm party tonight," Dylan said.

Malory didn't have any such dilemma. She only had

one swimsuit. But she was also planning on wearing a gorgeous emerald sarong that used to belong to her mom. It had been too long for her for the past year but now it finally fit perfectly.

She pulled the fruit salad towards her. As much as she didn't feel like eating, she'd need the energy for her riding session. *Not to mention an encounter with Caleb!*

Aiden Phillips was driving the short-listed students over to Allbrights. Ms Carmichael had left a little before with the horse van. Malory had helped load the horses, and Tybalt had walked on without a hint of stress. Malory crossed her fingers as she took a seat on the bus. She just hoped Tybalt's calm mood would last until the end of the riding session.

"So it's just the four of us who've been short-listed?" Antsey van Sweetering was the last one to get onto the bus. The freshman slid onto the seat in front of Malory and turned around to continue talking. "If Peanut knew that his lazy summer was at risk I bet he'd deliberately knock every jump down at the training sessions and give three refusals at the All Schools League Show."

Malory smiled. Printer's Apprentice, also known as Peanut, was Antsey's own pony. The chestnut gelding had a jump to rival a much bigger horse; Malory couldn't even picture him crashing his way out of the show.

"Don't worry, Antsey. Peanut loves competing. It's the ponies that don't have any experience at first-class competitions that I'm concerned about." Lynsey shot Malory a glance.

"If you're talking about Tybalt, then he's done great on his last couple of outings," Eleanor Dixon protested.

"Maybe." Lynsey shrugged. "But I think that if the Cavendish Foundation knew his history they'd reject him in a second."

Malory wanted to argue in Tybalt's defence but couldn't find the words. Lynsey was hitting too close to her own worries. But she was determined to get the best performance ever out of the brown gelding this afternoon. Actions always spoke louder than words, and if she had her way, Tybalt's performance would do all the talking.

The bus turned up the wide, tree-lined avenue that ran through the centre of the Allbrights campus. They passed outdoor tennis courts, a baseball diamond, and playing fields before reaching the sign pointing the way to the stables. The girls fell silent, and Malory wondered if they were finally feeling as nervous as she was. The butterflies in her stomach felt like they'd morphed into giant mutant moths.

They pulled into the parking lot, and the girls quickly scrambled off the bus. The horse vans were parked in a paved area at the side of a huge barn. Malory couldn't resist peeking through the open doors. A couple of girls were inside carrying tack. They gave Malory a friendly smile before disappearing down the aisle.

"Come on," Lynsey called impatiently.

Malory left the barn and hurried after Lynsey, Eleanor, and Antsey. They soon spotted the Chestnut

Hill truck. Ms Carmichael and Kelly had already un-loaded the horses and tied them at the side of the van.

Malory counted another three horse vans and a half dozen horse boxes. She looked for the Saint Kits truck and saw it on the other side of the lot with its ramp down. They must have arrived early, because there was no sign of the boys or their horses.

"I'm glad the horses are all clean under their travel sheets," Antsey said to Malory. "If I stayed out for long in this heat to groom them, I'd turn into a puddle on the ground – that's if the gnats didn't get me first." She slapped at a fly on her arm and then took a deep breath. "I know it's crazy, but I'm feeling as nervous as when I'm about to ride in a competition."

Malory nodded. "Me, too," she confessed. The sooner she began warming Tybalt up the better. She could always get a better grip on her nerves when she was in the saddle.

Ms Carmichael was unwrapping Bluegrass's travel bandages. "As soon as you're done, go to the indoor arena on the other side of the barn," she called out.

"OK." Malory nodded. Before unbuckling Tybalt's travel sheet she offered him a horse cookie from her pocket. "You're an absolute star. Show everyone how bright you can shine today, OK?" she murmured in his ear.

She buckled on her hard hat before mounting and took another quick glance around. Eleanor and Antsey were giving their girths a final check, and Lynsey was going over Bluegrass with a stable rubber.

"Lynsey, you can already see your face reflecting in his coat!" Ms Carmichael told her.

Malory could understand why Lynsey wanted Blue to look his best. All the other students had turned out their horses to show standard, even though this was only supposed to be a training session. It was clear that everyone was going all-out to get a spot in the programme. The atmosphere was going to be even more competitive once they were in the arena. *Which should suit Caleb just fine*, Malory caught herself thinking. She swung up into the saddle, determined not to think of Caleb during the session. She wanted to give one hundred per cent to her performance. She might not share the same fierce competitive streak as the other students but she still wanted to do her best, for Tybalt's sake as much as her own.

Malory rode into the large indoor arena behind Eleanor, who was riding Shamrock. The building was obviously newly constructed, with huge windows set behind the upper viewing gallery. Natural light poured in and gleamed off the white-painted boards around the perimeter of the ring.

Malory noticed Aiden Phillips and Ali Carmichael take a seat in the viewing gallery. She was suddenly distracted by Tybalt, who had laid back his ears and squealed. Malory glanced back to see that the rider behind had gotten too close.

"Sorry," a girl on a black mare apologized. "Hunter's worst habit is outpacing the horse in front."

Malory figured the Thoroughbred had to be nearly seventeen hands. She thought she recognized the horse and rider from an interschool competition. "You're from Wycliffe, right?"

The girl nodded. "My name's Helena Macey."

"Malory O'Neil." Malory smiled at Helena before twisting back in the saddle.

Out of the corner of her eye, she saw Caleb riding down the opposite side of the ring on his striking-looking grey. Pageant's Pride, otherwise known as Gent, had his neck arched gracefully. Malory wished she could get Tybalt so relaxed. Being overcrowded had upset him, and he felt really tense. She used her legs to encourage him to reach up into the bridle but Tybalt's stride remained short and uncomfortable. She tried giving and taking with the reins in the hope that Tybalt would drop his head, but he carried it stubbornly high, his jaw set against her hands.

"Everyone ride into the centre, please." Elizabeth Mitchell had walked into the arena without Malory noticing. She was dressed casually in jeans and a loose shirt but her brown eyes were shrewd and assessing.

Encouraging Tybalt away from the track, Malory hoped the gelding would stand quietly. She noticed Caleb halting Gent farther up the line and couldn't tell if she was relieved or disappointed that he hadn't chosen to stand alongside her.

"First off, I'd like to congratulate you all on being short-listed for the Cavendish Riding Programme. We could have future Olympians among us!"

Malory couldn't join in with the exchanged glances and smiles that broke out among the group of almost twenty students. She was too busy trying to calm Tybalt, who was pawing at the sawdust.

"He's just impatient to get going," Helena whispered, nodding at the grid that had been set out at the far end of the arena.

Malory smiled but she knew that it wasn't impatience that had Tybalt swishing his tail and fidgeting, it was anxiety. *None of the other horses seem stressed. What if Ms Mitchell tells the selectors that Tybalt doesn't seem cut out for this kind of pressure?*

"I've prepared name tags for you all, so when I shout out your name just put up your hand," Ms Mitchell announced.

When she came over to give Malory her sticky label, Ms Mitchell laid her hand on Tybalt's neck. "Boy, is he tense. His muscles are tying themselves up in knots. Put him at the back of the class and leave at least two horse lengths between you and the last rider. If he's got some space, he might recover some of his equilibrium."

Malory thanked her, relieved Ms Mitchell could see that Tybalt wasn't acting up out of naughtiness. When the class rejoined the track, she kept Tybalt back and quietly worked him between her legs and hands until he began to drop his head and lengthen his stride. By the time the class finished their warm-up, Tybalt was relaxed and responsive. Malory was the last to ride a three-loop serpentine and she couldn't help but smile proudly as Tybalt bent around her leg, his inside ear flicking back to show he was listening to her.

"Well done, Malory. I'd like you to ride the grid first, please," Elizabeth Mitchell called. Malory was grateful that the instructor didn't give Tybalt the opportunity to tense up again by being made to wait.

Aware of all the assembled students watching her, she snuck a quick glance at Caleb. He smiled over at her. Malory broke eye contact and looked between Tybalt's ears instead. She hoped Caleb wouldn't think she'd just snubbed him. She was so nervous, all she could do right now was focus on getting around the course.

She cantered Tybalt at the first fence, a cross pole, which would be followed by a succession of three single raised poles and then another cross pole to jump out of the grid. His mouth felt hard as he resisted her hands. But once he entered the takeoff zone before the first fence he relaxed and went obediently through the grid. Malory gave a sigh of relief as he popped over the final fence.

"I'm sure you're all thinking that I'm insulting you with such an easy task." Ms Mitchell's voice rang out. "But coming back to basics with your grid-work is essential to ironing out any faults your horse might develop during regular jumping practice." She walked towards the first placing pole in the grid and replaced it with a garish yellow-and-green-striped one. "Take him through again," she called to Malory.

The moment Tybalt saw the new, brightly coloured pole he faltered, just as he had at the yellow-and-black bar in their last jumping session. There was no way he wanted to jump into the grid with that waiting for him. At the last moment he swerved to the right, giving Malory a refusal.

She immediately circled back to the fence.

"Good call!" Ms Mitchell praised. "Bring him down to a trot and think in terms of impulsion over speed. Look to the end of the grid – don't drop your gaze down to the pole."

Malory nodded without taking her focus away from the line of fences. She rode firmly forward, thinking all the time about riding leg-into-hand. Tybalt began to back off from the grid again but she leaned back and drove him on. She felt a thrill of delight as he jumped into the grid and cleared each successive fence.

Helena Macey began to clap, and the rest of the students joined in.

"Well done," Ms Mitchell called. "Fall back in with the rest of the class and give him a breather."

Malory thought Elizabeth Mitchell had a great way of giving constructive advice. No one would match Ali Carmichael in her opinion, but it was good to have a fresh pair of eyes assessing her performance. It was becoming more and more clear what a fantastic opportunity it would be to get into the Cavendish Riding Programme. The instructors were going to be giving feedback to the Cavendish selectors at the end of each training session, and Malory realized she had all her fingers crossed that Ms Mitchell would see through Tybalt's initial nerves and appreciate the huge potential that could place him on the A-Level circuit.

Maybe I was wrong to think that Tybalt wouldn't cut it at the top. He deserves the chance to show just how talented he is, as much as any other horse in here.

"Do you need a hand?" Caleb walked across to where Malory was getting Tybalt ready for the journey back to Chestnut Hill.

"I'm just about done, thanks," she replied. She was working T-touch on the gelding to keep him calm before he was loaded into the van. She was thankful she had something to keep her busy while Caleb stood there; otherwise she knew her body would make it clear what an effect he had on her. She could feel her face get warm and her hands get shaky as he continued to stand there looking at her.

Caleb came around to stand by Tybalt's head. "Hey, fella," he said softly. He scratched Tybalt between his eyes, and the gelding let out a sigh.

Malory watched Caleb out of the corner of her eye and she felt the butterflies in her stomach wake up again. *Who am I trying to kid that I'm over him?* But that didn't erase the fact that they had totally different approaches to riding. *And riding is all our relationship was based on. I bet he would never have asked me out if I wasn't so good with horses.*

"The way you handle him is pretty awesome," Caleb told her. "He's a different horse from the one who spooked out at the interschool competition last fall."

Malory thought back to Tybalt's first show. He'd collided with Caleb's horse and been so stressed out that she'd had to take him out of the show.

"He's got so much talent, all he needed was a chance to prove himself," she said, feeling a glow of pride for the dark gelding.

"I'm glad you decided to go ahead with your application," Caleb said. He moved around from Tybalt's head to stand closer to Malory.

"Me, too," Malory replied. She braced herself as she looked up into his blue eyes, trying not to get lost in their sky-coloured depths.

Caleb took a deep breath. "I'm sorry if I screwed up when I said you'd be better off with Liz Mitchell as your riding coach. It's easy to pass judgment on someone you don't know, but if I'd stopped to think about it, I'd have known not to be so harsh on your instructor. It's obvious you all really like her and I should have butted out." He gave a half smile. "What do you say to moving on and putting that dumb argument behind us?"

Malory felt a pounding in her chest and a tightening in her stomach. While her heart was saying one thing, her head was telling her another. Caleb hadn't mentioned that he was wrong to put competition above people. All he'd said was that he was wrong to criticize someone who meant a lot to Malory and her friends. He still obviously thought that a Director of Riding like Elizabeth Mitchell would do a whole lot more for Chestnut Hill than Ali, implying that she was foolish for preferring Ms Carmichael instead.

Malory desperately wanted to turn the clock back to the way things were before the fight over Ms Carmichael, but she knew that couldn't happen.

"Sure, I'd really like to be friends with you again." She placed enough emphasis on the word *friends* for Caleb to understand that friendship was all she was prepared to offer.

A muscle jumped near Caleb's mouth, and Malory thought she saw his cheeks flush. "Whatever. That's cool. I guess I'll catch you around, then."

As she watched him walk away, she wanted to call him back and take back what she'd just said. She could tell it had surprised and hurt him. But there was no point. It was clear they could never get back to the way they were before.

Malory sighed. All she could do now was turn in the performance of her life at the All Schools League Show. Not just to win a place in the riding programme, but to prove to Caleb that Ms Carmichael had more going for her than just popularity.

"You're back! How did the riding session go?" Lani was sitting on her bed, holding still while Honey painted her toenails.

"Did Ms Mitchell give good pointers?" Dylan chimed in. She was kneeling behind Lani, whose hair she was twisting up into a high ponytail for the dorm party. They'd been having a fashion fest by the look of the bikinis, tank tops, and sarongs piled on the bed.

Honey turned around, unaware of the drop of nail polish about to fall off the brush onto the carpet. Malory was going to warn her when Honey dunked the brush back into the bottle. "Did you get to speak to Caleb?"

"Whoa!" Malory held up her hands. "Which question do you want me to answer first?"

"The Caleb one!" the girls chorused.

"Do I get to shower before the interrogation?"

"Nope." Dylan patted the bedspread beside her. "Come on, tell us everything."

"Guys, I look like something that's just emerged from Dracula's crypt!" Lani said. She gestured to her half-painted maroon nails. "You can't leave me like this."

"I hate to sound harsh, but I think you need to get a professional stylist. Making you look good is just too tough for us," Dylan teased. "Otherwise, you'll just have to accept that you're a lost cause."

"With you as a friend, it's a good thing I don't have any self-esteem issues," Lani retorted.

"Always here to keep you grounded," Dylan replied smoothly. "So, come on, Mal. What happened?"

"I think I might have messed up big-time." Malory felt relieved the moment the words were out. Maybe her friends could help her get a handle on what had just gone on between her and Caleb.

"Did Tybalt freak out?" Lani asked.

"No, I mean I messed up with Caleb, not the lesson.

That was pretty cool – Ms Mitchell sure lived up to her reputation."

"Why do you think you went wrong with Caleb?" Honey prompted.

"He came to see me after the lesson and apologized for what he said about Ms Carmichael. He asked if we could move on and I more or less told him I just wanted to be friends."

"Um, was the emphasis on *more* or on *less*?" Dylan asked, swapping glances with Lani.

"More." Malory grabbed the cushion beside her and covered her face.

"But why?" Honey gently pulled down the cushion. "Have you given up on the idea of getting back together with him?"

"I must have, since that's what I told him."

"OK, Mal, I want you to lie back." Dylan jumped off the bed and dragged a chair up close. She crossed her legs and held out an imaginary pen and paper. "I think we should start with your childhood. It's OK, you can tell me everything."

"Not funny!" Malory threw the cushion at Dylan.

"I think you still really like him, but you're worried that he's not the person you fell for last summer," Honey said seriously.

"Yep, you've got a bad case of the jitters and you're putting up barriers higher and faster than Qin Shi Huangdi's crew," Lani said, dropping in a reference to their latest history unit on the Great Wall of China.

Malory nodded. "I guess I'm afraid that Caleb's only

interested in the Malory who has the talent to win prizes."

"You're worried he doesn't know the real you." Dylan nodded. "And the only thing the two of you have in common is riding – and that's starting to fall apart now that it's obvious that he's in it for the winning and you're not." Dylan stroked her chin as she continued. "You're backing off from spending more time with him because you can't face the reality of it ending in a tragedy. Better to *think* that might happen, than to actually experience it."

Lani looked impressed. "Wow. Where did *that* come from, Dr Phil?"

"Huh? It came right out without me even thinking about it." Dylan pretended to look amazed but couldn't hide a grin. "I think I just found my calling."

"Mal, Dylan is right. You're never going to know for sure how things are going to turn out unless you give Caleb a chance." Honey put her hand on Malory's arm. "You'll regret it if you don't, and I know that he's anxious to give things another shot. Josh told me that Caleb's planning on inviting someone from the seventh grade to the formal. That has to be you!"

Malory absentmindedly tugged at a piece of hay caught in her hair. "I don't know. He's been practically ignoring me for the last few weeks. Asking me to the formal is pretty major. He only suggested moving on today. I think he wanted to take things slowly."

An awful thought struck her. "Oh, my gosh! Maybe he's dating another girl. Maybe when he mentioned moving on he was talking about with someone else! And I assumed he was asking me to be his girlfriend again." She pressed her hands against her burning cheeks. "He must think I'm an egomaniac!"

Chapter Six

Malory side-tied her sarong over her aquamarine swimsuit.

"That really brings out the colour of your eyes," Dylan said admiringly.

"Thanks." Malory smiled and checked Dylan out. "You look . . . interesting."

"Do you think it's overkill?" Dylan wriggled her hips, swishing her Hawaiian grass skirt. She wore silk-flower garlands around her ankles, neck, and wrists.

"Um, not really." Malory didn't want to tell her she looked like an advertisement for a greenhouse after Dylan had gone to so much effort.

"Bummer. I knew I should have bought more garlands. If you can't go over the top for an end-of-year dorm party, then when can you?" She pulled off the shirt she was wearing. "Maybe this will help," she grinned, looking down at her bikini top.

"Where did you get that?" Malory exploded with laughter loud enough for Honey and Lani to poke their heads out of the adjoining bathroom door.

Dylan pirouetted so they could all get a good look at the top that was patterned to look like a pair of coconut shells.

"Don't they know the meaning of the word 'style' in Virginia?" Lani teased.

"Hey, my friend, we keep reinventing it, but don't worry, the rest of the country catches up in time," Dylan shot back.

"I think you'll find the rest of the country taking a rain check on this particular fashion statement," Lani said as Dylan pulled on a long black wig to complete the look.

"I never figured you for a killjoy, Hernandez," Dylan said.

"Just trying to stop you from committing social suicide," Lani replied.

"I think the flowers are a great idea," Honey said, walking over to examine the leis around Dylan's neck.

"Did you hear that? She thinks they're a great idea," Dylan echoed, looking smug.

Honey bent down to pretend to smell the flowers, and before Dylan could react, she had swiftly pulled out one of the pink orchids. She took a barrett from the dressing table and used it to pin the flower just above her ear.

"I've been plucked!" Dylan exclaimed.

"I knew my outfit was missing something." Malory advanced on her friend and sized up one of the blue silk flowers.

"Back off," Dylan warned, holding up her fingers to form a cross. "No cannibalizing my look."

Malory slicked on the Ruby & Millie lip gloss Mrs Harper had given them and then turned to face the others. "Let's go party!"

They heard the party before they saw it. The bass of the blasting music could be heard halfway across campus. They walked across the lawn and over to the sports centre. The centre had an indoor pool so the girls could swim year-round, but Malory preferred the outdoor pool. There were individual shower and changing rooms built against the back of the complex. The patio area in front of them was shaded by a roof supported on neoclassical pillars. A few steps led down to the pool area, which was decorated for the party with plastic palm trees and beach umbrellas.

It looked as if just about all of the Adams girls had arrived and most of them were in the pool, where a crazy game of volleyball was going on.

"Our party is going to be the best out of all the dorMs I know that Meyer House is throwing a dance in the school hall. How lame is that compared with this?" Lani said, waving her hand in the direction of the pool.

"Oh, my gosh," Lynsey said loudly as she walked past with Patience. Both girls were staring at Dylan. "Phone nine-nine-nine quick! There's a fashion victim in need of emergency treatment."

"Chill out, Lynz," Dylan said, for once not rising to the bait. "How 'bout we have a time-out just for tonight? We can put the sparring gloves back on in the morning."

Lynsey's eyebrows shot up. "Fine by me. Although it's been more like firearms lately."

"Admit it, you wouldn't have it any other way." Dylan grinned.

Noel and Alessandra were in charge of the barbecue and were already turning hot dogs and burgers. Malory's mouth watered as she caught a whiff of fried onions.

"Yum, tacos," Dylan said. She pointed at a table that was set out with more food.

"Check out the catering!" Malory exclaimed as she eyed the marinated chicken, rolls, chips and dips, and ice cream standing in boxes of ice. On another table were coolers stocked full of fruit kebabs, smoothies, and sodas. With the sun still beating down, she felt more like having a cold drink than eating. She chose a soda and drank it quickly. She couldn't wait to get into the pool with the rest of the girls. She'd eat later; the last thing she wanted was a cramp from eating just before swimming.

When the girls emerged from the pool, wet, drippy, and laughing, the game was finished, and Malory had worked up a real appetite. She loaded up a paper plate with a cheeseburger, chips, and a soda and then joined the others on the deck chairs.

"I can't believe how fast this year has gone by," she commented as she took a bite out of her burger. The ketchup she'd piled onto her roll escaped down her chin.

"Yeah, I can still picture you crawling on the ground like a mutant tortoise trying to get Nutmeg to come near you." Dylan grinned, handing her a napkin.

Malory remembered back to that first day. "Well, at least I managed to catch her!"

"And I thought Honey was going to be sucked over to the Dark Side at first," Dylan continued.

Honey was picking the radishes out of her salad. "What do you mean?"

"Lynsey and Patience thought your English accent was just *fabulous* and got all friendly with you right from the start. I bet Patience was hoping to get an invite to spend a holiday hanging out with you so she could meet Prince William."

Honey rolled her eyes. "As if."

"You know, this has got to be the best party yet," Malory remarked. She loved the themed sea shapes that had been taped to the changing room doors. The seahorse was her favourite.

"You say that about every party," Wei Lin teased as she and Razina sat down. She balanced her plate on her knee while she rubbed sunblock onto her arMs "Noel asked me to spread the word that the seniors have a surprise for us before the movie."

"I guess they've decided it's so awesome here they're going to refuse to graduate. It means that we'll never get to move up grades and we'll have to stay in the seventh grade forever. Madame Dubois will still be shouting at us for getting our verbs wrong when our hair's turned grey and we have dentures," Lani said.

"The ponies will be using walkers by then." Malory giggled at the mental picture of Tybalt pushing a walker with his front legs.

"So, Raz, what are your plans for this holiday?" Honey asked. "Will you be spending time travelling?

Razina's mom owned an art gallery, and her dad was an entertainment lawyer. Malory knew it was often difficult for them to coordinate time off together, so Razina travelled a lot with one or the other during the holidays.

"My mom's taking me on a cruise to see the Norwegian fjords for a couple of weeks, but for the rest of the summer I'll be helping her at work," Razina said. "She's thinking of opening a new gallery in Boston, which should be pretty exciting. I've been trying to persuade Wei Lin to spend some of the holiday with us. She's got an amazing eye for design."

"My parents want to take me sailing on our yacht, but they're not sure how much time they'll be able to take off from work," Wei Lin explained. Her mom was the financial director of a banking company and her dad was a majorly important eye surgeon. "When their plans are finalized I'll have a better idea of how much free time I'll have."

Malory knew that the idea of taking part in the Cavendish Riding Programme must seem just as exciting to her friends as opening a new gallery or cruising in Scandinavia. But she still felt unsettled about leaving her dad for the entire summer. *Everyone's planning to spend time with their families except for me.*

"Have you finished eating? The seniors want to move over to the lawn," Alexandra came to tell them.

"Ah, the surprise." Lani got up and brushed crumbs off her lap. "Lead the way."

The seniors were waiting on the lawn where they were going to watch the movie. There was a projector and giant screen all set up and ready to go. Malory noticed that most of the seniors were holding wrapped packages.

"Oh, they're going to do the 'Last Will and Testament,'" Lynsey said as the lower school sat down. "My sisters told me all about this. It's when the seniors hand something down to the first-years."

"Cool," Lani said. "I hope I get the popcorn-making machine from their common room."

"Actually, it's just personal stuff they give out," Patience said.

Lani rolled her eyes. "Duh, irony is just wasted on some people."

Holly Leigh-Barber, editor of *View from the Hill*, the weekly student-run newspaper, cleared her throat. "I don't know if everyone in the seventh grade knows how this works, but basically, before we seniors leave, we like to give something to the first-years for you to remember us by. Alex," she smiled at Alexandra, "this is for you." She held out a small, slim package.

Alexandra turned bright red and stumbled on her flip-flop when she stood up to walk over to the seniors.

Holly waited for her to tear the paper off. "You submitted a great article last week that we're going to run in the last edition of the term. I think you've got a real talent for writing."

Malory felt delighted for Alex, who was staring down at Holly's vintage silver fountain pen in amazement.

"I wrote my first article with that pen," Holly explained. "It was a piece on a mother-and-daughter fashion show we put on in my last term as a seventh-grader. I want you to have it, to carry on the great tradition of feature writing at *View from the Hill*."

Alexandra looked up, her eyes shining. "Thank you so much," she gasped.

"My turn," Noel said. She looked across at Lani and pretended to toss something to her.

Lani went along with the charade and acted like she'd caught the object. She then put on a look of total bemusement as she opened her hands to see that nothing was there.

"On second thought, you'd better come up here for it," said Noel. "I don't doubt your catching, but my pitching has been way off this semester."

Lani walked up to the seniors and took the round, brightly wrapped gift from their dorm president. She tore off the paper and held up a weathered-looking - softball.

"This is my lucky ball. I always practise with it before any game," Noel said. "I hope it helps you hit even more home runs."

"This is amazing, thanks," Lani said, turning the ball over in her hands.

Dylan put her fingers in her mouth and let out a piercing wolf whistle.

"Go, Lani!" Malory called as her friend walked back, tossing the softball into the air and catching it.

Next, Alessandra di Schiapari stood up and called Malory forward.

Malory felt her cheeks burn. It hadn't occurred to her that she might be called up.

"I'm going to give you something that isn't actually mine," Alessandra began with a smile.

"Hey, we don't want anyone to get busted for handling stolen goods," Dylan teased.

"Don't worry, that's not going to happen," Alessandra assured her. She looked at Malory, her brown eyes earnest. "It's always been a tradition at Chestnut Hill for a senior rider to pass this on to a seventh-grader." She held up a worn horseshoe. "Alicia Mayfield, who was captain of the senior team when I started, gave it to me. It belonged to Miss Dawtry, who founded Chestnut Hill."

Malory stared at the worn crescent of silver metal, gleaming in the dusky light.

"It belonged to Miss Dawtry's Arabian mare, Lace," Alessandra explained. "We see it as a symbol for the importance of horses here at Chestnut Hill. Every time I look at it I think about how much they achieve for the school and how much we owe them in return." She smiled broadly. "I can't think of a better pair of hands for it to go to." Alessandra presented the shoe to Malory and the girls broke into applause.

"Wow," Malory swallowed. "Thank you." She pictured the horseshoe propped on her nightstand so that it would be the first thing she'd see in the morning and the last thing at night. She felt a thrill of delight as she ran her fingers over the shoe, noting the old scuff marks that must have been made by Lace cantering over the campus. A painting of the beautiful chestnut mare hung in the foyer of the Old House. Malory tried to get her head around the fact that she was actually holding one of her shoes!

"One of the reasons I decided to give you the shoe is because you've always seemed more concerned about connecting to the horses than competing," Alessandra explained. "And that's exactly the way Miss Dawtry was. Apparently, once, in the middle of winter, she slept for a night in the barn with Lace, who was recovering from a bout of colic. It didn't matter to her that she had an emergency meeting with the Board of Governors the next morning. Rumour has it that she turned up late with pieces of straw in her hair!"

Malory's fingers closed around the smooth, polished metal, feeling a tingling at the back of her neck to know that other girls had done exactly the same ever since Chestnut Hill had begun. "Thank you. I promise I'll take really good care of it until it's time to pass it on to somebody else."

Alessandra's eyes were warm. "I know you will."

The other seniors gave out their gifts but Malory could barely take her eyes off the shoe. Honey got a framed snapshot of the campus in the fall, and Dylan inherited a subscription to *Vogue* magazine. "To help guide you in your fashion forward lifestyle," Jessica Anderson said, laughing as she handed over the envelope to the hula-clad Dylan.

"We'd better get this movie going before we run out of time," Noel announced at last.

"You're not thinking of putting that horseshoe on Tybalt's stall door, are you?" Lynsey asked on her way past Malory to take her seat for the movie. "He's hardly the best reflection of the school's equestrian tradition."

Malory winced. Lynsey was clearly put out that she hadn't been given the horseshoe.

"Didn't you like your gift?" she asked mildly. Lynsey had been given a smoothie maker from India Drakakis.

"Oh, please, like I'm going to make my own smoothies when I can buy them from the student centre," Lynsey said witheringly.

Malory didn't say anything. There was no point in provoking any more antagonism. If they both ended up in the Cavendish Riding Programme, then a hostile Lynsey could make for a pretty uncomfortable summer holiday.

"Do you think it's possible to just be positive for a change?" Lani said pointedly to Lynsey. "Try thinking of something nice – like diamond earrings in your party-favour bag."

"I can think of plenty of reasons to be cheerful," Patience retorted. She turned to look at Lynsey, but it was clear her comment was meant for Malory's ears. "At the top of my list is that Caleb's going to invite me to the formal."

Malory's chest tightened and she suddenly found it hard to breathe. She was relieved when Lani stepped in.

"Do you know, I don't think we'll be able to hear the movie over all the noise pollution here," her friend said icily as she glared at Patience.

Dylan and Honey stood closer to Malory and slipped their arms through hers.

"Come on, Patience, let's go get a decent seat for the movie," Lynsey said with a smirk.

Malory raised her chin, determined that Patience and Lynsey not see how wounded she was by the news. But as they walked off, their satisfied smiles told her they knew just how shaken she was by the bombshell Patience had just dropped.

Malory sat through the movie without taking in a single word. She felt like her stomach was filled with cement. *Caleb is going to ask Patience to the formal.* She had shredded an entire patch of grass by the time the credits rolled. She knew that her friends hadn't paid much attention to the film, either. They'd been too busy shooting her anxious glances. Malory appreciated how much they cared about her feelings, but she just didn't feel like talking.

By now it was dark and hundreds of white fairy lights twinkled in the trees that fringed the lawn. As the movie ended and the music came back on, Malory muttered to Dylan that she was going to get a drink, but sped off down to the paddocks instead.

Peering into the semidarkness, she could see the silhouettes of horses grazing but couldn't pick out Tybalt. She gave a whistle and immediately one of the horses threw up his head. With a low whicker, Tybalt trotted over to the gate. For once he didn't snuffle her hands for treats but stood like a rock while she leaned against him, drawing comfort from his warm, solid presence. It looked like her suspicions were right – Caleb hadn't been trying to make up with her – he was getting back together with Patience.

"How am I going to face him at the training session tomorrow?" she asked miserably. It didn't matter that Tybalt couldn't reply. *I'll just act like he doesn't matter to me.*

But she knew deep down that he did. And she was afraid that the truth would be as clear to everyone else as it was to her.

Chapter Seven

"Open, Tyb," Malory encouraged. She slipped her finger into the back of the pony's mouth to get him to take the bit. With reluctance, Tybalt opened his mouth and the bit grazed over his teeth as Malory slipped his bridle on.

Malory knew that the gelding had to be picking up on her negative vibes. She was totally freaked out by the whole Caleb and Patience revelation from the night before and it was coming off her in waves.

"Hey, Mal, there's an urgent phone call that you need to take in Ms Carmichael's office. I'll finish tacking Tybalt up for you." Sarah slid back the bolt on Tybalt's stall and stepped in.

"An urgent call?" Malory felt her heart skip a beat.

"It's your dad," Sarah nodded. "He said there was nothing for you to worry about," she called after Malory as she raced up the barn aisle.

Malory snatched up the phone receiver that was lying on Ms Carmichael's desk. "Dad, what's wrong?" she panted.

"Hey, sweetheart. I said that there's nothing for you to worry about," her dad, sounding totally normal, replied.

"I was told it was urgent." Malory was still worried.

"I just wanted to let you know that there was a little trouble at the store last night," her dad told her. "I waited until after your lessons, but I forgot you had extra riding practice. When the receptionist told me you were in your lesson I tried to tell her I'd call back, but by then she'd already put me through to Ms Carmichael's phone. Sorry, hon. I shouldn't have said it was urgent."

"What kind of trouble was there?" Malory asked, feeling a light sweat break out on her palms that had nothing to do with the fact that she'd sprinted all the way from the barn.

"It's all being taken care of and I don't want you to worry about it, OK? I want you giving one hundred per cent to your lesson today."

"What kind of trouble?" Malory asked again, ignoring his instructions not to worry. Her anxiety was increasing with every second.

"We had a small break-in," her dad told her.

"A break-in? Are you all right?" Alarm rocketed through Malory. Her dad lived above the store. He could have been hurt.

"I'm fine," Mr O'Neil said quickly. "They forced their way in the back door of the store and managed to make quite a mess before I got down there and chased them off."

"You chased them?" Malory half shouted. "How many of them were there? Why didn't you stay upstairs and call the police? They could have had a gun, Dad!" *I've already lost one parent. How could you do this to me?* she thought in a panic. She took a deep breath. "I'm coming home right now."

"Sweetheart, I don't want you to do that. I was afraid if I called you'd freak out," her father said. "But I knew you'd be even more upset if I hid it from you. Listen, there's nothing you can do here."

"How can I think about school when you've just been robbed?"

"The police have already been over to take a statement. Everything's fine here and I'm getting new security installed. My insurance will cover everything that was stolen or destroyed. I don't want to keep you up from your lesson any more so we'll talk later, OK?"

But as Malory hung up she realized there was no way she was going to be able to concentrate on anything other than her dad. *He was all on his own when the break-in happened. That's the way it is for him now.* She felt a heaviness settle on her that she knew wouldn't be easily shaken off.

"Easy, Tyb," Malory said as Tybalt tossed his head and broke into a restless trot. She brought him back to a walk and tried to focus on her riding instead of thinking about her dad.

It was the Monday before the All Schools League Show and the second training session for the Cavendish

Riding Pro-gram was taking place that evening. Each of the schools' instructors was taking a turn at training the candidates and reporting on their performances, and tonight it was Ali Carmichael's turn. They were using both outdoor arenas for flatwork and jumping. The class was already warming up by the time Malory halted at the arena gate and reined Tybalt back to open it. When she rode through and indicated to Tybalt to turn on the forehand so she could shut the gate, he resisted, swishing his tail crossly and sticking his nose in the air. Malory knew there was no point in trying to force him to obey as he would only end up getting even more stressed. She knew he was picking up on her tension but she just couldn't get herself to relax.

She rode around the arena, using transitions between walk and trot to get his attention. Tybalt wouldn't settle so she turned him off the outside track to ride a serpentine, but halfway through she found herself on the wrong diagonal. Tybalt broke into a few strides of canter, thrown off balance.

"Easy, boy," Malory said apologetically. She just couldn't get a grip on her riding. All she kept thinking about was her dad, all alone at home, right above the store as it was being ransacked.

Helena Macey flashed a smile as she rode past on Hunter. The big black mare covered the long side of the school in an easy relaxed stride. Tybalt's steps seemed short by comparison. Malory used her legs to encourage him to lengthen his stride, but Tybalt just laid back his ears and tried to go faster.

A showy grey was cantering down the opposite side of the arena. *Gent!* Malory's heart jumped into her throat and she couldn't help looking at Caleb, but he avoided making eye contact with her as he slowed Gent into a working trot.

After a while Ms Carmichael asked everyone to work on a twenty-meter circle. Malory groaned. This was exactly the sort of exercise that would wind Tybalt up with the mood he was in. *Get a grip, O'Neil,* she told herself. She concentrated on using her legs behind the girth to encourage him to bend properly around the circle. Just as Tybalt began to flex correctly, Malory caught sight of Patience walking down to the arena wearing her favourite lemon-coloured Julian McDonald minidress. Patience leaned up against the fence and waved across at Caleb.

Oh, come on! Does she really need to be here? Malory thought in annoyance.

The moment Malory's attention wandered, Tybalt veered into the circle. She tried to get him working correctly again, but she was fighting a losing battle as the gelding resisted her.

By the time they moved to the jumping arena, Tybalt was wet with sweat and foam was dripping from his bit. He hadn't been this worked up since he first came to Chestnut Hill.

"Everyone warm up over the practice pole before we take a look at the course," Ms Carmichael called out. While Malory was waiting her turn, her instructor walked up to her and laid her hand on Tybalt's neck.

"What's wrong with him today?"

"I don't think my mind's totally on what I'm doing," Malory admitted, shortening her reins as Tybalt pawed at the ground. "I just got a call from my dad to say the store was broken into last night. I keep thinking of what might have happened to him."

"No wonder you're distracted." Ms Carmichael's voice was full of concern. "I know this is going to be tough but do your best to settle him. Don't forget that these training sessions count towards the final decision. Your selection isn't just based on your performance at the show. But I'll make sure I report that you've had recent family problems on any notes I make about how you ride today." She paused. "And will you send my best wishes to your dad?"

Malory nodded. She understood that Ms Carmichael was keeping her best interests at heart. *But right now I'm not sure that the riding programme is my best interest; being with my dad is.*

When it was her turn, she rode Tybalt strongly towards the pole. But despite her determination, Tybalt's forelegs rattled the pole and sent it thudding onto the sandy surface. Malory glanced across at Ms Carmichael to see if she wanted them to take the fence again, but her instructor waved her over to join the group.

Ms Carmichael had them all line up facing the far end of the arena where eight fences were set out. "Whatever course you're riding, it's important that you use a mixture of forward driving aids and restraining

116

aids. Think about rhythm and straightness, and don't forget to use half-halts for balance." She paused and ran her eyes over the group. "But the most important thing to remember is that you're one half of a partnership. Your horse is not a machine; he'll have his good and bad days, just like you. It's important that he can put his trust in you and your judgment, so you can work together even when things aren't going your way."

She waved her hand towards the course of jumps. "Today I want to concentrate on the track before, between, and after the fences. Don't forget that horses don't see a fence clearly when they're really close to it so it's not fair to expect them to negotiate the jump if they haven't had a chance to size it up."

She nodded at Lynsey to ride first. As she turned Bluegrass to face the fence, Ms Carmichael called, "Collect, weight, turn, and push!"

Bluegrass's hocks engaged, and Malory saw his power increase as he came off the forehand. "When you ride the turn properly, it can be used to improve your horse's balance," Ms Carmichael told the students. "Lynsey should have selected the right spot for takeoff by now." Bluegrass's stride shortened, and Lynsey sat deep in her saddle for the final three strides. "At this point, with any fence, you need to allow your horse to concentrate on negotiating his way. Use your hands to invite him to stretch forward and maintain your forward signals."

Bluegrass's takeoff was perfect and he formed a gorgeous bascule as he cleared the jump. Lynsey shifted her weight to encourage Bluegrass to land on the correct canter lead for the next fence.

"See how Lynsey used her forward signals as soon as Blue landed," Ms Carmichael commented. "She didn't drop any contact and immediately set him up for his next fence."

That's how I need to ride Tybalt, Malory thought, *always one stride ahead of him*.

When Lynsey rejoined the group, Ms Carmichael congratulated her. "One of Lynsey's strengths is that she rides Bluegrass quietly. What I mean by that is she doesn't make any exaggerated movements when he takes his fences. You'll all have your own individual riding styles but the less you interfere with your horse as he's going over a fence, the more likely you'll be to get a clear."

Lynsey looked pleased as she leaned forward to pat Bluegrass's neck.

Caleb rode next, and Malory couldn't help admiring the way he handled the grey gelding. Patience was the first to applaud when Gent cleared the last fence and returned to the group in a beautiful, collected canter.

Caleb glanced across at Malory. She met his gaze and held it. *How could you go back to Patience?* The accusation shouted in her head. Malory felt her hands form tight fists.

Caleb dropped the eye contact like he had heard the question.

"OK, Malory." Ms Carmichael nodded for her to go.

Malory tried to ride just the way her instructor had

advised but when she turned the corner towards the parallel she could feel Tybalt was on his forehand. She rode deep, but instead of responding by bringing his hocks under him, Tybalt began shaking his head in protest. He swung his quarters out and was cantering at an angle as they approached the fence. Malory didn't even attempt to get him over but rode straight past.

"Bring him around again," Ms Carmichael told her.

Malory knew that his stride was completely wrong as they entered the takeoff zone this time. Tybalt managed to stop from actually crashing through the pole but that didn't prevent Malory falling onto his neck. Feeling mortified, she pushed herself back into the saddle and gathered up her reins again.

She didn't look at Caleb but could sense his eyes fixed on her. She felt a wave of anger. She didn't need his pity!

Her instructor waved her back. "I know there's a good reason why Tybalt's not in a jumping mood today and I don't want to stress him out any further. It's not good for him to end his session on a refusal, though. Take him up to the other end of the school and try him over the practice jump. Once you've gone over it, reward him, and then take him back to the barn."

Malory nodded, her cheeks on fire. She gritted her teeth as she cantered Tybalt up to the practice fence and rode him with maximum impulsion. Tybalt responded by clearing the pole, and Malory gave him a quick pat on the neck before riding him to the gate.

Patience ran to hold it open. "That was awful!" she exclaimed.

"Thanks," Malory said sarcastically. "I would never have figured that out without your experienced appraisal."

Patience's eyes widened. "Oh, my gosh, I didn't mean you!"

Yeah, right, Malory thought.

"I mean, *you* can't help it that Tybalt's totally unreliable."

Malory bit back an angry response. She'd already stressed Tybalt out; she wasn't about to make it worse by getting into it with Patience.

She rode past without another word. The truth was, she was so mad at herself she didn't have any anger to spare for anyone else. She knew that Ms Carmichael was right when she said there was a good reason behind their poor performance, but as far as Malory was concerned there was no reason good enough when it came to letting Tybalt down. She didn't deserve the horse-shoe Alessandra had given her the night before. The senior had said that it represented all that the horses achieved for the school and what they were owed in return.

And here I am letting my personal feelings interfere with my riding. Tybalt deserves much more than that.

Malory massaged lavender oil into Tybalt's coat and spoke soothingly to him.

"Hey, you're finished early." Dylan stopped outside

the stall. She was swinging Morello's halter. "How did it go?"

"Terrible," Malory groaned. She kept working the oil with her fingers, glad to see Tybalt stretch his nose out to blow in a friendly way at Dylan. He seemed to have shaken off his earlier tension. "My mind wasn't on it, and Tybalt got really stressed out. I feel like such a jerk." She didn't feel ready to confide in Dylan about the break-in yet. She'd rather do that somewhere less public.

"Hmm," Dylan said sympathetically. "Listen, I promised Kelly I'd rinse Morello's water bucket but I'll be right back so you can tell me all about it, OK?"

Malory appreciated Dylan's concern, but as her friend walked away she knew that all she wanted to do was forget the lesson as quickly as possible. Despite the fact that Ms Carmichael was going to make a note about the reason for her poor performance, she had probably blown any chance she had of getting into the Cavendish Programme. *But I don't even care about that right now. How can I possibly leave Dad alone for the summer?* Her father would always be number one in her life and she'd be spending the summer with him.

"That horse is out of control!" cried Lynsey as she stalked up to the door and pointed a finger at Tybalt. "There's no way he's reliable enough to be part of the junior jumping team."

"Thanks, Lynsey. I was feeling really upbeat about today until you came to offer some constructive criticism. If you hadn't, I'd have walked away thinking we'd done just fine," Malory snapped.

"He's got no place on any competitive outing. You'll turn us into a laughingstock," Lynsey continued.

Malory's heart sank when she saw Caleb appear behind Lynsey. He must have heard every word.

"Ms Carmichael had better change her mind about allowing Tybalt on the team if we want to stand any chance of placing at the show." Lynsey spun on her heel. "I'm going to talk to her about it right now."

Caleb waited until Lynsey had gone before he spoke. "Bad luck, today." He scuffed the floor with his boot. Malory could see he was feeling awkward and she wondered if he had found out that she knew about him and Patience.

Malory shrugged. She wasn't about to tell him the news about her dad, let alone how rattled she was about him getting back together with Patience. *The girl he'd said wasn't his type!*

Caleb rested his arms on the low wall. "You know, I think Lynsey might be right about riding Tybalt at the All Schools League Show." He paused. "Do you think you should consider taking a different horse on the programme if you get selected? You're such an amazing rider, if you teamed up with the right horse you could be incredible."

"Thanks, but I don't see horses, or *people*, in terms of what I can get out of them," Malory said bitingly. "If Tybalt doesn't turn out to be a winning ticket, I'm not going to toss him away. But that's because my focus isn't on the end prize, it's on enjoying the journey." Just because she was having doubts about the riding programme didn't mean she was going to let anyone put Tybalt down.

"You'd enjoy the journey even more on a more reliable horse that's got the right mind-set for competition," Caleb pointed out.

"Yeah, well, some of us don't give up on things as easily as others," she said, her tone loaded with double meaning. Why couldn't he just go back to Patience and leave her alone?

Caleb stared at her and then shrugged. "Suit yourself. But I'm telling you, Mal, Tybalt's not cut out for the A-Level circuit."

Malory stared after him in furious amazement. When it came to being thick-headed, Caleb wrote the book!

Chapter Eight

"Wow, you sure told Caleb. I wish I'd been there to hear it." Dylan let out a long whistle. "Although it's pretty weird having you guys fight. You seemed so right for each other when you first got together. I hope it's not catching. I'd hate Henri and me to start going at it like that. I can't imagine how hard it is."

Malory plucked at a loose thread on Dylan's bedspread. They'd both gone up to her dorm room to talk after seeing to the horses. Malory wanted to point out to Dylan that she and Henri hadn't even been on a real date yet, but she didn't want to sound petty. *If I'd been as confident in my relationship with Caleb as Dylan is about Henri maybe I'd be even more upset now.* But she still couldn't shake off her suspicion that Dylan was reading more into the relationship with Henri than the older boy intended.

"I guess one of the reasons I really lost it with Caleb was because I was already upset. I got a phone call from my dad just before the practice session. His store got broken into last night," Malory told her friend.

"No!" Dylan exclaimed. "That's awful. Are you OK? Is your dad OK?" She fired the questions out before giving Malory an impetuous hug.

"Everyone's OK. "Thanks, Dyl." Malory appreciated her friend's -concern.

Dylan gave her another big squeeze.

Malory dropped eye contact with her friend and began to wind the loose thread around her finger again. "I'm hoping you're going to understand my decision about the Cavendish Foundation."

"Huh? Did I miss something?" Dylan frowned. "What decision?"

"I'm not one-hundred-per-cent-sure I'm going to go ahead with my application," Malory admitted. "I don't want to make a knee-jerk reaction about the break-in, but it's rattled me big-time. I feel like all I want to do is be with my dad this summer. He's so important to me, and it's bad enough that I'm away from him during school without going away for the summer as well."

"It sounds like you've made up your mind to me," Dylan said bluntly, not sounding particularly pleased about Malory's decision.

Malory shook her head. "I really don't know what to do. I'll definitely finish the training programme since we've only got a couple more sessions. Tybalt deserves that much at least – especially after I let him down today. I really want to prove to the others what a great performer he can be when he gets a fair chance."

"And what about you?" Dylan questioned. "Do you

think you're giving your riding career a fair chance by dropping out of the programme?"

Malory glanced up to see that her friend's eyes were full of concern. "I'm just torn. I know that nobody will be more disappointed than my dad if I do decide to drop out. But there's something deep inside me that's telling me to stay at home this summer." She made a helpless gesture with her hands. "I just wish I knew for sure what to do."

Later that night, Malory slipped over to the student centre to check her email. She logged on and saw she had one email waiting from the day before. It was from Amy Fleming! Since Amy had come to Chestnut Hill to help out with Tybalt's rehabilitation she and Malory had swapped notes about the gelding's progress. Malory propped her elbows on the workstation and leaned closer to the screen.

Hey, Mal – I'm home for the weekend, but I wanted to make a quick reply to your last email. I'm really glad Tybalt is continuing to respond to his treatment. Like I said, though, any troubled horse's recovery depends just as much on the owner's dedication and belief as on any alternative remedies!

The new cross-country course sounds great. Maybe I can finagle an invite to its official opening? I'd love to take Sundance over – he adores flying over the jumps Joni and I built on one of our trail routes. Did I tell you that Joni is one of the stable hands here? I don't know what would happen to Heartland if it wasn't for her dedication – and Ty's.

Malory knew Ty was the head stable hand. She stopped reading for a moment and tried to picture him but the only image she could come up with was Caleb. Malory rolled her eyes at herself. Why was it that thoughts of Caleb were always pushing their way into her head? She turned her attention back to the final line of Amy's email.

Got to run, there's a whole barn of stalls to be mucked out! Take care,
   Amy ☺

Malory quickly typed out a reply to Amy's email and then, in the final paragraph, mentioned the Cavendish Riding Programme. She felt a little awkward sharing her personal problems with the older girl. But she really trusted Amy's instincts. Just look what she'd done for Tybalt. And Amy's mom had died a few years ago, too. She'd be able to empathize with how torn Malory was feeling between taking a place on the riding programme and being with her family. As much as Malory's friends were great to confide in, they couldn't relate to her need to be with her dad. Amy's reply would be more balanced and might help Malory arrive at the right answer.

The junior jumping team had a practice session every day during the week leading up to the All Schools

League Show. Tybalt had turned in a great performance each day, despite Malory's doubts about continuing with the Cavendish Programme.

On Thursday evening, the training session for the Cavendish students was held at Saint Kits. Malory was confident she'd show Caleb how wrong he was about Tybalt. During the warm-up, she kept her attention totally on the gelding. She hadn't so much as glanced at any of the other riders, and Tybalt had calmly obeyed every command.

She watched as Lynsey and Bluegrass finished the course of six jumps set up in the outdoor arena. So far during the lesson, every student had brought down the stile halfway around the course. Lynsey didn't look pleased as she took her place back with the other students. The stile was set at a tricky distance out of a turn, and Malory knew she'd have to get Tybalt on the right lead at warp speed so she could concentrate on measuring his stride up to the fence.

"Are you ready, Malory?" called Mike Burnell, Saint Kits's Director of Riding.

Malory shortened her reins and sent Tybalt forward. The gelding responded with a smooth transition from walk straight into canter. They cleared the upright, the parallel, and the spread. When he landed after the wall, Malory turned him as sharply as she could to set up a good line for the stile. As they approached the fence and Malory chose her takeoff mark, she encouraged Tybalt to put in an extra short stride. She felt a moment of euphoria as he sailed over the stile. They landed clear, and Tybalt gave a small, playful buck as the watching students burst into applause.

"That was very well ridden. Be careful that you don't get overconfident and end up shaving too much off the turns," Mike Burnell warned, "but that was a great performance."

Malory felt thrilled. She knew Tybalt had just turned in a class act that proved he did have it in him to be on the A-Level circuit. *Even if I decide not to go ahead with the riding programme, Tybalt's just shown that he's got every right to be there.* As they trotted back to the group, she refused to look at Lynsey and Caleb, Tybalt's loudest critics. The dark brown gelding's performance had sent out a message so loud and clear that she didn't feel the need to add anything to it!

Back at Chestnut Hill, Malory rubbed Tybalt down and gave him extra carrots in his feed as a reward for his performance.

After she had turned Tybalt out into the paddock she decided to go check her email in the student centre.

When she logged on to her account she saw that she had an email waiting from Amy. With a feeling of anticipation, Malory opened the mail and began to read.

It's wonderful news about the riding programme but it sounds as if it's got you feeling pretty torn. I know you were looking forward to being with your dad this summer but riding the A-Level circuit is an incredible opportunity. I bet you feel like you're caught up in a spin cycle choosing where to be this summer.

I can't tell you what to do, Mal. All I can say is that I understand how you must feel. After my mom died, home and family became a million times more important to me. Right now, you must want to grab every minute you can to be with your dad. The Cavendish Riding Programme would be an awesome experience, but if you turn it down that doesn't mean you're shutting the door on other amazing chances that may come along in the future. I believe family memories are priceless – and I know that you'll understand where I'm coming from when you read this.

That's not to say that you should panic for the rest of your life, living every minute as if it could be your last. My advice is to strike a balance. Although I guess that at this moment, balance is hard to find. You either go in the programme or go home to be with your dad.

Sorry I couldn't be of more help!

Let me know what you end up deciding,

Amy

Malory read the email through twice. Even though Amy wasn't telling her one way or the other which way to go, her words had made the choice much more clear. There was no balance if she decided to go in the programme. She'd be leaving her dad for the summer and there was no way around that. But if she stayed home, she could still come up to the school and continue with Tybalt's training and who knows what other opportunities could come from that in the future?

I'm going to stay home with Dad. Even as she thought the words, it was as if a heavy weight was lifted off her shoulders. They could spend the summer doing all the things they'd originally planned. Riding opportunities would come and go, but this summer was reserved for her father.

Malory pushed back her chair from the desk. She couldn't wait to go call her dad and tell him her decision.

"Hi, Mal." Her dad sounded pleased to hear her.

"Hey, Dad." Malory decided to get straight to the point. "I'm calling with some news." She took a deep breath. "I've decided not to go ahead with the Cavendish Programme."

The silence was so long at the other end of the phone that Malory thought they'd been cut off. "Dad?"

"What made you drop out? You were so excited about it." Her dad sounded bemused.

Malory fiddled with the phone cord. "I'd be away for most of the summer and I don't want to spend that long apart from you. It's not like I'm in a regular school where we see each other every night."

"There'll be other summers."

"That's what I thought about Mom," Malory whispered.

Mr O'Neil took in a sharp breath. "Is that why you don't want to go on with the riding programme?

Sweetheart, you can't spend your life thinking that way."

"But I'd really miss you." Malory felt her throat close.

"I'd miss you, too, of course I would," her dad admitted. "But the reason you're at Chestnut Hill is because of your talent. It's a gift, Malory, and you should do everything in your power to make the most of it." He paused. "Your mom would have wanted you to go for it."

"Mom would have wanted what was right for us as a family, and that's being together," Malory said firmly.

"Sweetheart, I don't want you to miss out on this opportunity. If it's me you're worried about, you should know that I'm absolutely fine. We're going to have a new alarm system installed, if it makes you feel any better—"

"Dad, it's not just because of the break-in," Malory said. The last thing she wanted was for her father to blame himself. "I just know that the time isn't right for me to be going in for intensive competitive training." It was only a year ago that she'd been riding at the local level. So much had happened in the past twelve months that she wanted the summer just to catch her breath. And even though she'd had an awesome year with her friends, she wanted to have time with her dad now. "Please, say you understand."

She could tell by his voice that he was smiling. "Call me selfish but I can't help liking the idea of having my daughter spend the summer with me." He hesitated.

"Just promise me one thing – that you've taken time out to really think this through."

Malory laughed. "I've done nothing but think it through all week!" She paused. "I love you, Dad."

"I love you, too, sweetheart. And I'm more proud of you now than I've ever been. Your mom would feel the same if she were here. Our lovely, precious daughter."

Malory fought against the lump in her throat as she hung up. She'd made the right decision. But she was still going to go all-out at the All Schools League Show to help bring home the trophy for Chestnut Hill. Even if she wasn't competing for a spot in the Cavendish Programme, the school had given her so much in the last year, this was her opportunity to give something back.

Malory groped from under her pillow for her alarm and switched it off. This was way too early to be awake! She snuggled back under her blanket and tried to slip back into the dream she'd been having about cantering Tybalt down a stretch of golden beach. Suddenly she remembered why she'd set her alarm so early. *The All Schools League Show!*

She shot upright. She had a zillion things to do to get ready. First she needed to go down to the yard to bring Tybalt in from the field and groom him. Although Ms Carmichael usually oversaw the ponies' preparation, Malory had asked permission to see to Tybalt. She wanted to do T-touch to get him into a calm and relaxed mood. Then she'd have to have breakfast and get changed into her riding clothes.

She pulled on her yard clothes and shook Lani by the shoulder to wake her up.

"Today's the day," she whispered when Lani blinked sleepily at her. "I'll see you down in the barn."

She padded catlike past Alexandra, who was still fast asleep, and slipped through the door before hurrying down the corridor.

"Up, Tyb," Malory encouraged when the gelding refused to pick up his leg. She took a firmer grip on the hoof pick. She didn't blame him for not cooperating. She'd dropped the body brush three times while she was grooming and it was clear Tybalt was starting to pick up on her nerves.

It had been bad enough letting Tybalt down during the practice session at the start of the week but to let him down before the big show was unthinkable. She needed to come through for Tybalt because she owed it to him, plus she wanted to do well to prove what a great instructor Ms Carmichael was. Finally, she longed to turn in a great performance for the school. Maybe if she started working some lavender oil into his coat it would have a calming effect on her, too! Malory finished picking out Tybalt's hooves and went to get the oil from the tack room.

"Where's Mermaid's martingale?" Elyn Sachs-Cohen asked, frantically rummaging through the tack box. "I know I left it on his bridle hook after I cleaned it last night."

"There's a running martingale on top of one of the bins in the feed room," Paris Mackenzie told her as she scooped up Whisper's tack.

"That's where it is!" Elyn exclaimed. She handed back the martingale she'd been holding. "This one must be yours. I found it on the floor and was going to use it for Mermaid."

"It's a good thing I found yours, then, or I'd be riding the course with Whisper's ears in my face," Paris told her.

Malory couldn't help smiling. Every morning before a show even the most levelheaded riders went a little crazy. Before long, Ms Carmichael, Sarah, and Kelly would be chasing them out of the yard so some order could be restored.

She took her bottle of lavender oil off the shelf and left the room just as Antsey van Sweetering hurried in muttering, "Head collar, head collar."

We should have a sprinkler system put in, fill it with lavender oil, and set it to spray us all each time we get ready for a show! As she returned to see to Tybalt, Malory hummed a melody her mom had used to sing to her at bedtime when she was little. A sense of calm settled over her as she began to massage the oil into Tybalt's coat, and a phrase that her mom had once said snuck into her mind: *If wishes were horses, then beggars would ride.* Well, if wishes counted for anything then, coupled with all the intensive training the Chestnut Hill teams had put in over the past weeks, they would be bringing home the trophies for sure!

* * *

"Here, let me help." Honey reached up and gently swatted Malory's hands away. She untangled Malory's tie before neatly re-knotting it for her.

"Thanks," Malory said, folding down her shirt collar. She looked around the room. "Where did I put my hat?"

"Here." Dylan rescued it from the top of the laundry basket. She and the others were already dressed in their show breeches, white shirts, and school ties. Honey and Lani were riding in the show as well, which had classes open to all riders. Lani had entered Colorado in a speed-jumping round, and Honey was riding Minnie in a preliminary dressage class.

"I'm all done," Malory said. "Thanks, guys."

Lani nodded at the yard-stained jodhpurs Malory was wearing. "Um, I'm not sure you're going to impress the Cavendish selectors wearing those."

Malory stared at her friend in dismay. She had come to her decision so late last night that she hadn't had a chance to tell anyone but Dylan that she was dropping off of the short list. She hadn't even told the Cavendish Foundation.

"Deep breaths," Honey advised her speechless friend as she unhooked a pair of white breeches that had been cleaned for the show off the back of the door.

I'll have to tell them after the show. They'll never agree with my decision and now is not the time to go into it.

Lani stuck her hand out. "Team Chestnut Hill!"

Dylan placed her hand on top of Lani's and echoed the chant. Honey did the same.

137

Malory was the last to join in, and as soon as her hand touched theirs, they changed the chant to a victory call. *"Go, Chestnut Hill, go!"*

Malory handed Honey the hoof oil so she could brush a final coat over Minnie's hooves. The Connemara Arab cross was looking around the busy showground at Allbrights with her ears pricked. Malory imagined a thought bubble above the mare's head saying *Let's go!* It was clear from her bright eyes that she was totally relaxed and ready to compete.

The Chestnut Hill trucks were parked at the top end of the field against a tall hedge for shelter. The sun was beating down, and the flies were out en masse. Malory had sprayed Tybalt from head to tail with repellent, but as she slapped at a fly on her arm she felt relieved they'd be competing indoors.

"Can you hold the stirrup on the other side while I mount?" Honey asked.

Malory nodded and pulled down on the stirrup to keep the weight even on the saddle as Honey swung up onto Minnie's back.

"Sam and your parents just got here," Lani called as she jogged up holding bottles of drinking water. "They went over to get ringside seats. Sam said he's going to bribe the referee on our behalf!"

Honey rolled her eyes. "Maybe you should go back and tell him that if he sees a man walking around in a black-and-white-striped shirt with a whistle around his neck, he's more than welcome to try and bribe him, but if not, then I'll just try and turn in a good performance for the judges."

Dylan rode around from the other side of the truck on Morello. "Hey, guys. Rumour has it that Dr Starling's coming to watch."

"It's more than a rumour." Kelly, who was helping with the show, walked up with Malory's hat. "You left this on the bus," she said.

"Thanks." Malory slipped it on.

"You'd better get moving if you're going to get these horses warmed up before their classes," Kelly warned them.

"Did you see my dad when you went to get the drinks?" Malory asked Lani. "He's coming to watch."

She shook her head. "No, sorry. There're hundreds of people out there."

Malory mounted Tybalt and checked his girth before riding across the field with Dylan. The rest of the junior team had already gone over to the collecting ring with Ms Carmichael. Malory lost count of the horse trailers and trucks that were parked all over the field. She stood in her stirrups to get a glimpse of the adjacent field where the other riding classes were taking place. The end-of-year event was huge!

She was about to join the line for the practice pole when Ms Carmichael walked up and put her hand on Tybalt's neck. "How are you doing?"

"I could do with a focus pill," Malory admitted, feeling her stomach twist with nerves.

Tybalt took a few steps back and swished his tail.

"Steady, boy," Malory soothed.

"Look, the practice pole is free now. Why not take him over to keep his mind occupied?" Ms Carmichael suggested.

The gelding stood well back from the fence and jumped large. Malory was slightly unseated but she kept her balance and made sure she didn't jab his mouth when they landed. "Good boy." She patted his neck.

"He looks raring to go," Ms Carmichael said when Malory rode back to her. "Bring him over to join the others."

Lynsey, Eleanor, Olivia, and Dylan were waiting in the far corner of the collecting ring. Even though Dylan was team reserve, she was mounted on Morello for the Open Jumping Class, which was taking place later.

"OK, you know from when we walked the course earlier that there's nothing out there you haven't come across in our training sessions," Ms Carmichael said briskly. "Don't do anything differently, and you'll be fine. If any fence is going to be scary, it's the upright after the water. You're going to need to increase the pace to get enough spread over the water and, if you're not careful, you're not going to get your balance back in time to clear the upright following it."

Malory was distracted by a well-dressed middle-aged couple walking by with clipboards. She swapped a glance with Lynsey. Could they be the Cavendish Foundation scouts? If so, maybe she should go tell them that she was dropping out of the programme. Lynsey shrugged her shoulders as if Malory had spoken the question out loud. *I can't go over unless I know for sure who they are*, Malory thought worriedly. It was also bugging her that she hadn't informed her instructor of her decision. She knew Ms Carmichael would be disappointed, but Malory hoped she would understand where she was coming from.

The Saint Kits riders had gathered around their instructor on the opposite side of the collecting ring. Caleb was mounted on Gent, looking very professional in his dark blue jacket and spotless white breeches. The grey horse looked like something out of a legend with his gleaming silver coat and long silky mane and tail. *Shadowfax*. Malory thought he could have come straight out of *The Lord of the Rings*. Caleb put his leg forward so he could lift his saddle flap to tighten his girth.

As Caleb bent down to fix the buckle, Malory saw Patience walk up with a bottle of water. Their heads were so close, they were almost touching. Malory used her leg behind the girth to push Tybalt around so they wouldn't be in her field of vision.

"Watch it," Lynsey snapped as Tybalt got too close to Bluegrass and laid his ears flat at the blue roan.

Malory nudged Tybalt over and tried to tune back in to Ms Carmichael's final instructions as the first rider's name was called over the PA system.

"You're up!" Dylan exclaimed.

"Huh?" Malory hadn't realized it was her name being called.

"Good luck, Malory. Just concentrate on a nice rhythmic pace," Ms Carmichael said, stepping back for her to ride past.

This is it, Malory thought as she squeezed Tybalt forward. *This is my chance to give something back to Chestnut Hill and to show what Tybalt can really do.*

Chapter Nine

Malory's fingers tightened on the reins as she rode by Patience and Caleb. Tybalt picked up on her tension and skittered sideways.

"Here we go; Malory serves up another embarrassment for Chestnut Hill. Do you think she'll get past the third fence before scratching this time?" Patience said to Caleb, loudly enough for Malory to hear.

Malory felt a surge of anger wash over her. How dare *Patience* judge *her* riding? Tybalt had earned his place on the junior jumping team as much as any horse! The round ahead was the chance for Malory to silence his critics once and for all.

Everything became a blur as she rode into the arena. The bleachers behind the plastic screen that circled the arena were full of supporters, but Malory was only semi-aware of them. Tybalt had her total concentration, and at that moment, nothing else mattered besides partnering him around the course.

For one scary moment she felt as if she'd never jumped a fence in her life. Then they cantered across the starting line and instinct kicked in. As they took the first fence Malory had a glimpse of what it must be like to ride a push-button horse. Tybalt did everything perfectly. His approach, takeoff, outline, and landing were flawless. As if to prove he wasn't a push-button, he tried to rush the second fence but Malory knew it was from enthusiasm, not nerves. *He's really enjoying himself!*

Tybalt soared over the parallel but skipped a step when he landed. Malory quickly collected him to try to regain his beautiful rhythmic pace. Tybalt stood back from the third fence, and Malory guessed the edge had been taken off his confidence. *Come on, Tyb,* she willed him, driving him forward. Tybalt took off a fraction too late but Malory was ready for him and didn't get in front of the movement. They landed in unison and Malory began to prepare for the next jump – the water.

As they turned the corner and cantered towards the jump she could almost feel Tybalt's eyes popping at the brightly coloured potted plants that edged the shallow plastic pool. She urged him to go faster and felt Tybalt spring forward with a flat but generous jump. She wasn't worried about his back legs going into the water as much as the change of pace he'd need to make before the next jump.

When Tybalt landed clear of the water she sat deep to get his hocks engaged so he'd be able to make the height of the upright. She heard the crowd groan as Tybalt took off too early and rattled the top pole with his hindlegs. *Please stay on.*

Malory didn't know if the pole had fallen or not but she didn't dare look behind as she and Tybalt tackled the wall and cantered on to the final fence, a double. She could feel Tybalt sitting back, spooking at the red-and-yellow fillers. Malory closed her legs against him, knowing she couldn't risk overriding him and having him flatten the fences.

Tybalt hesitated only slightly before he jumped the first fence. Malory had already paced out three strides when she'd walked the course earlier but Tybalt took her by surprise when he landed short. She sent him forward to increase his pace and to her relief he took off perfectly for the final part of the double.

The arena erupted into applause.

"Malory O'Neil on Tybalt for Chestnut Hill rides clear," the announcement came through on the speakers.

A clear round! She rubbed Tybalt's neck as they cantered towards the exit. He'd been totally amazing.

As Malory rode Tybalt out of the ring, she saw Caleb trotting towards her on Gent. "Amazing!" He flashed her a smile as they passed each other.

Malory was so surprised that she didn't have a chance to wish him luck.

"Well done!" Ms Carmichael congratulated her as she rejoined the team. "That certainly set a high standard."

"You guys looked incredible out there!" Eleanor exclaimed.

"Yeah, I've never seen Tybalt look so responsive. He

looked picture-perfect over every fence," Olivia added.

Even Lynsey managed some grudging praise. "You almost couldn't tell what a menace that horse is."

Malory ignored the barb in Lynsey's comment. She knew Tybalt had finally shown everyone that he had been worth the effort to get him this far. The beautiful dark gelding arched his neck as she pulled off her stirrups and jumped down. She loosened his girth and ran up her stirrups, realizing that if the rest of the team rode well they might have a real chance of placing!

Kelly came up with a rug to throw over Tybalt's quarters. "That was fantastic!" she congratulated Malory.

"Wasn't Tybalt amazing?" Malory felt ready to burst with pride.

As Caleb trotted out of the ring, the announcement came over the PA that he had turned in a clear round. Malory watched out of the corner of her eye as he was greeted by his team members with high fives.

An Allbrights competitor was next up, and she rode out with the first faults of the competition from Ms Carmichael's scary fence.

"Their winning streak is looking a bit shaky," Dylan said with a glint in her eye.

"Beware the commentator's curse," Malory told her.

"Huh?"

"As soon as you say they're not doing great they'll start doing perfectly," Malory said.

"Oops! Well, in that case, Allbrights is amazing. Go, Allbrights, go!" Dylan pretended to panic.

"I'd better go cool Tybalt down," Malory said with a smile. She would be able to walk the gelding up and down the far side of the collecting ring and still listen to the results of the rounds as they came in.

"Hang on," said Eleanor. She pulled Skylark closer and reached down to touch the top of Malory's shoulder. "Just in case some of your luck can rub off." She smiled.

"Malory O'Neil?" The well-dressed middle-aged woman whom Malory had spotted earlier approached her as she walked Tybalt away from the group. She wore low-heeled leather boots and tan slacks with a hint of equestrian tailoring.

Malory halted Tybalt. "That's me."

The woman ran her hand down Tybalt's neck. "You did very well out there," she said.

"Thanks, Tybalt was great," Malory agreed, feeling a warm glow of pride in the beautiful gelding.

"You both were." The woman held out her hand. "I'm Victoria Golding from the Cavendish Foundation."

"Hi." Malory realized her initial guess had been right. At least she could let the selectors know of her decision now so they could cut her out of their decision-making process.

"We were very impressed with your round. We've been told something of Tybalt's history from your riding instructor, and his improvement is remarkable."

"Thank you," Malory said, slightly stunned.

The scout smiled at Malory. "Based on the feedback we've had from your training sessions and your performance today, I'm pleased to let you know that we'll be offering you a place on our summer riding programme. You'll need to wait for official confirmation in the mail, but I thought you'd like to know how well you've done."

Malory felt a surge of elation that she and Tybalt had been selected. But that was enough for her. She was content to spend her summer with her dad.

Tybalt pushed against her with his nose, telling Malory that he wanted to get moving again. Malory rubbed him between his eyes, carefully choosing her words. Finally she looked up at Ms Golding.

"I really appreciate the opportunity. It's amazing. But I'm afraid I'm not going to be able to participate this year."

Ms Golding frowned. "Has something happened?"

"I only made up my mind late last night," Malory explained. "So I haven't had a chance to let the Foundation know. It's for personal reasons, but it's been an honor to take part in the selection process."

Ms Golding hesitated and then held out her hand. "I know I'm biased, but I don't know of any other riding programme that matches ours. Why don't you discuss your decision with your instructor and your parents. I hope that when the offer arrives, you'll check off the acceptance box."

As Malory watched the scout walk away she felt the same calm settle over her that she had when she'd first decided not to go ahead with the programme. She was going home for the summer, where she belonged.

Malory turned her attention back to Tybalt. "Now, if I can only find a way to spend some time with you over the summer, everything will be perfect," she whispered to the pony.

"Hey, that was a great round."

Malory turned to see Caleb leading Gent towards her. *Well, almost everything*, Malory thought.

"Do you mind if I walk him around with you?"

Yes, I do mind, Malory wanted to say. *Go walk Gent with Patience and her Gucci stilettos.* But what came out of her mouth was, "Sure."

"You and Tybalt really looked good today," Caleb complimented her.

"Thanks. You're allowed to say you were wrong about him." Malory tried to make it sound like she was teasing, but she meant every word. Caleb owed Tybalt a major apology.

"I'm glad he proved me wrong today, but that doesn't mean I'm wrong about his temperament. I still don't think you should take him in the Cavendish Riding Programme."

Malory took in a sharp breath but Caleb carried on. "One of their scouts just came over and offered me a place!" His eyes shone, making them even bluer than before. "I saw her speaking to you first. Will you be there this summer, too?"

Malory shook her head.

Caleb looked genuinely dismayed. "I'm really sorry. I thought you were a shoo-in. Did she tell you why you didn't make it?"

"I did make it," Malory told him. "But I turned the place down."

"You did what?" Caleb raised his voice, making Gent throw his head up and snort. "You can't be serious!"

"I am," Malory said. "I have other things I need to do this summer."

"More important things than riding the A-Level circuit?"

"There are plenty of more important things than competitions," Malory replied.

Caleb stared at her. "So does that mean you turned the place down to make some sort of point?"

Malory stared back. How did she ever think she and Caleb were on the same wavelength? "Of course not."

"I don't get you." Caleb shook his head.

"Funny, that's just what I was thinking," Malory quipped.

Caleb ran his hand through his hair. "I'd like to say I'll see you around, but I guess that's not going to happen, right?"

"Not this summer," she agreed.

Caleb looked at her for a moment longer. Then he shrugged and turned to go.

As she watched Caleb walk away, she felt a tug of regret, remembering the great time they'd had together the summer before. So much had changed for the better for Malory during the past twelve months, but one thing she wished had stayed the same was her friendship with Caleb.

Malory led Tybalt back to the rest of the junior jumping team just as Eleanor was trotting into the arena. She rode clear until she came to the upright after the water. The crowd groaned as Skylark brought the top pole down. Although the team captain went clear over the remaining fences, she still looked unhappy when she rode out.

"I can't believe I didn't have her collected in time," she said as she dismounted. She patted Skylark's shoulder. "It wasn't your fault, girl."

"Don't beat yourself up over one knockdown," said Ms Carmichael. "You and Skylark did a great job out there. We're in third place at the moment, with Allbrights and Saint Kits tied for first. They're only three points up on us so we can still take the lead." She held Skylark while Eleanor ran up her irons and loosened the girth.

"I'll go cool her down." Eleanor clicked her tongue to the chestnut mare.

Malory decided to take Tybalt back to the truck so she could get back to the arena and watch the rest of the jumping. Dylan offered to go with her and, leaving Morello with Ms Carmichael, they walked Tybalt away from the collecting ring, past the main showground, and into the field where the vehicles were parked.

Malory decided there wouldn't be a better time to tell her friend she really wasn't going ahead with the Cavendish Programme.

Dylan was quiet for a moment. "What made you finally decide?"

Malory had been expecting Dylan to be upset just like Caleb. "It's mainly because I need to be with Dad more than I need to be in the programme," she said. "But I also really don't feel like the time is right for me or for Tybalt to be competing so heavily."

"Yeah, right. Anyone watching you two in action today could see that," Dylan teased. Then her voice got serious. "I just want what's best for you, and since you know yourself just a teeny bit better than I do" – she held up her hand to measure a millimeter – "then I won't try to talk you out of it."

Malory felt a surge of appreciation for her friend. Caleb may not get her, but Dylan certainly did.

Just then, Dylan's BlackBerry beeped. She pulled the handset out of her pocket. "It's Henri," she grinned. "Honestly, he just can't get enough of me!"

I wish I could say the same of Caleb, Malory thought as Dylan scanned her message.

"Is everything OK?" she asked when her friend stopped dead in her tracks.

Dylan didn't reply. She handed over her BlackBerry without a word.

Malory read the brief message.

Might have to rethink my summer visit. Have been asked to go on European tour by fabulous girl I met at school. Wish me luck! Will email with more details later – I know you'll be dying to know all. Henri.

"New love interest?" Malory repeated. "But I thought you and he were. . ."

"Well," Dylan started as she kicked at a divot. "I guess I may have been playing things up a little. I kind of knew I was a little young for him." She paused to glance at Malory. "But it was more fun to think of him *that* way."

Malory would never have guessed that Dylan also suspected that Henri never thought of her as a girlfriend. And, as impressed as she was by her friend's ability to be lighthearted about things, that didn't mean that her friend wasn't hurting like she was over Caleb. "I'm really sorry," she said, slipping her arm through Dylan's. "Are you going to be OK?"

Dylan shrugged. "I was kind of hoping he would turn up for the formal." She gave Malory a mischievous smile. "But I guess the chances of him flying in from France were pretty small – even if he *was* my boyfriend."

Malory grinned back at her. "I guess you're just going to have to slum it with us single gals," she told her.

"We might start the night off without a date, but we won't end it that way," Dylan said, tilting her chin with determination. "Not if I've got anything to do with it!"

Malory could tell her friend was hurting and that her nonchalance was an act. She respected Dylan's right to deal with the rejection in her own way and didn't push her any further. But as far as Malory was concerned, if she wasn't going with Caleb then she'd rather not think about getting together with anyone else. Boys were clearly more effort than they were worth!

When they reached the truck where there were buckets of water set out, Malory offered Tybalt a short drink before tying him up with a hay net. Sarah was sitting on the lowered ramp, keeping an eye on the senior team's horses, which were all tacked up and ready for their class. "How's it going?" she asked.

"We're in third place," Malory told her.

The seniors were heading across the field, ready to begin warming up.

"Hey, Mal, great round." Alessandra came over to them. "We saw Olivia ride just now and she went clear, too."

"We're still in it to place!" Dylan cheered.

Alessandra nodded. "I'd say there's going to be more than one placement to come out of today." She raised her eyebrows meaningfully at Malory.

"Actually, I've already turned the place down," Malory said. She figured she'd have to get used to apologizing to all the people who'd persuaded her to apply. "I really appreciate the great advice you gave me, though."

"That's no problem. Just for the record, pressuring you into taking up the place wasn't what I was trying to do. At the end of the day, you're the only one qualified to decide whether it was right for you." Alessandra smiled. "And with your talent, I'm sure you'll have plenty of other chances come your way."

Malory felt a rush of gratitude that the senior was able to empathize with the way she was feeling.

"So you won't be repossessing the horseshoe?" Dylan joked.

Alessandra pretended to think about it for a moment and then shook her head. "If it wasn't for you, Tybalt would probably have ended up at some auction house with all of that amazing potential never to be discovered." She squeezed Malory's arm. "I can't think of anyone else who deserves that horseshoe as much as you do."

Malory and Dylan found seats three rows back from the ring in the main arena. Caro Starkey from Allbrights was halfway around the course on her pony Razorbill.

"They're not going to clear the upright," Dylan murmured as Razorbill skipped when he landed after the water.

Malory nodded. The iron grey didn't have the balance to clear the upright and she wasn't surprised when the gelding ran out to the side. Caro circled Razorbill and rode him strongly at the fence, using her crop when the horse hesitated.

The angle was too tight and, although the gelding did his best to clear it, he still brought down the top pole with his forelegs. Rattled by the bad jump, Razorbill hit a block out of the wall, but recovered for the double and finished the course with six faults.

Lynsey was the last competitor to ride. Bluegrass looked every inch a top show pony as he cantered into the ring. He and Lynsey made a striking pair – and

Malory had to admit they were impressively competent. She timed the water jump perfectly so Bluegrass was fully balanced as he faced the upright, his hindlegs engaged to give a powerful jump over the fence. Lynsey was already looking over to the wall. *One, two, three*, Malory counted Bluegrass's strides before the fence. He cleared it effortlessly before sailing over the double. Malory and Dylan leaped up to applaud as Lynsey and Bluegrass cantered out of the ring.

"And that clear round from Lynsey Harrison on Bluegrass puts Chestnut Hill into second place. The final results are: Saint Christopher's, first place, Chestnut Hill second, Allbrights, third, with Wycliffe taking fourth," the voice over the PA announced.

Malory and Dylan threw their arms around each other. "Second! We came in second!" Dylan shouted.

They left their seats and raced around to the collecting ring. Lynsey had already dismounted and was talking with Victoria Golding, and Malory guessed from Lynsey's flushed expression that she was being offered a place on the riding programme. *She totally deserves it*, Malory thought fairly.

She looked around for Ms Carmichael.

"She's over there." Dylan pointed to where their instructor was standing a few metres away. "Isn't that your dad with her?"

Malory's heart flipped at the sight of the familiar dark-haired figure. "It is!" She hurried over to her father and gave him a huge hug.

"I just snuck in to tell you how wonderful your ride

was. I'm so proud of you, sweetheart." Her dad hugged her back, his brown eyes shining.

"Thanks, Dad." Malory felt that she was going to burst with happiness. There was just one more hurdle to get out of the way. She turned to face her instructor. "I want you to know that I passed the final selection for the Cavendish Programme. . ."

"That's wonderful!" Ms Carmichael exclaimed.

"But I turned the place down," Malory said in a rush. "I want to go home this summer. And, if it's OK with you, I'd like to come up to the school once in a while to keep working with Tybalt."

Ali was looking serious. "I think by now you've earned the right to have us put our confidence in your decisions," her instructor told her. "And I've got a feeling that Tybalt will do better with a quiet summer than a pressured couple of months on the A-Level circuit. So, as long as you are totally sure about this, then you have my support. I don't think I'm being presumptuous when I say that I'm sure you'll have other great offers in the future."

Mr O'Neil slipped his arm around her shoulder and hugged her to him again. Malory felt her heart fill with emotion for her dad, who had only ever given her his complete support. It must have been so hard letting her go away to school but he'd never once complained. Because of her dad's selflessness, she'd entered a whole new world, but the thought of an entire holiday spent in her old world was suddenly something she couldn't wait for.

* * *

The ribbons weren't being presented until all the teams had jumped and the Open Jumping was the last class of the day, so Dylan and Malory had plenty of time to go over to the showground. Mr O'Neil had stayed behind to get Ms Carmichael a coffee while she waited at the indoor arena for the seniors to jump.

Lani's class had already finished, and she and Sam were in line for hot dogs. "Honey's not riding for another twenty minutes so we thought we'd grab something to eat. Sam needs to eat every sixty minutes or his survival is threatened." Lani grinned.

"It's true," Sam nodded, biting into his roll. "I'm thinking of moving my bedroom down into the kitchen. It would be so much easier than taking the stairs eight times a night."

"I've often thought that I should have an en suite kitchen instead of a bathroom," Dylan said enthusiastically.

"How about we head over to Honey's ring while you guys are talking renovations?" Malory suggested.

"So how did you guys do?" Lani asked as they walked through the crowded showground.

"Second place," Dylan grinned.

"No way!" Lani exclaimed. She grabbed Malory and Dylan in a huge hug. "That's amazing."

"Seems like it's seconds all around," said Sam. "Lani got a blue ribbon for speed-jumping. See, I do know something about horses," he added, tugging the visor of his cap farther down against the sun's glare.

"Yeah? I'd better not tell them you thought

159

Colorado's fly fringe was used to make him go faster, then," Lani teased.

Mr and Mrs Harper had saved seats for them at the side of the dressage ring. They all quieted down while they waited for Honey to ride.

When her friend trotted down the centre line, Malory thought how great she looked in her black coat and white gloves, sitting in a perfect classical seat on Minnie.

"What the heck has she done to her horse's mane?" Sam asked in a whisper.

"She plaited it," Malory told him in a low voice.

"It looks weird," Sam decided, frowning.

Malory didn't reply. She was too busy concentrating on Minnie's medium trot. When the mare turned down the centre line, Malory noticed she went onto the forehand. After a few strides, Honey had Minnie working off her hindquarters again and looking collected and balanced as she circled on a ten-meter diameter. Minnie looked relaxed and supple as she rode the circle on one rein and then the other. Anyone watching them would think they had been a team for years, not months.

"She looks fabulous," Mrs Harper said softly.

Malory nodded, feeling very proud of her friend as she trotted down the centre line to finish. Minnie stood squarely without moving until Honey squeezed her forward and rode out of the ring.

Malory rushed with the others to the entrance of the ring to congratulate Honey. "That was amazing,"

Malory told her as she dismounted.

"Wasn't she terrific?" Honey said, hugging Minnie, who snuffled at her hand.

"We'd better run," Dylan said suddenly. "We need to get the horses and get back to the arena."

"You placed?" Honey asked.

"Second," Dylan told her.

"That's fantastic!" Honey said, her eyes shining.

"Hopefully we'll be able to get back in time to see you get your ribbon," Malory put in.

"Thanks, but I don't think there's much chance of me placing in this class," Honey said modestly. "I'm up against some tough competition."

"We'll see." Malory smiled. If Dylan did well in the Open Jumping later it could mean they'd all be going home with ribbons.

Chapter Ten

Malory glanced at her watch. She was supposed to be meeting up with the others in Honey and Dylan's dorm room at three. They'd planned on needing nearly four hours to get ready for the formal that night. But Malory wanted to slip down to the barn one more time to give Tybalt a horse cookie and thank him for his performance the day before.

She smiled when she saw Tybalt looking over his stall door. She'd never felt more proud than when she'd received her second place ribbon and cantered around the arena on the beautiful dark gelding who had tried his heart out for her.

Honey had come away with a blue ribbon, and Dylan had placed fourth in the Open Jumping. It had been an amazing end to their first year.

Tybalt whickered when Malory let herself into his stall. She fed him a mint, and as he crunched on it she wished he could talk and reassure her that he would be glad to stay at home this summer. She leaned her head against his neck and realized that not so long ago she'd have been able to talk the whole thing over with Caleb. *But not any more.* She sighed. It didn't matter how much they'd disagreed and how much she didn't like his fierce competitive streak, she knew that she couldn't ever hate him. In fact, she had to admit she kind of respected his dedication to his riding, even if his goals were different than her own.

The more she thought about Caleb, the more she realized that, despite their differences, she still really cared about him.

"How am I going to cope with seeing Patience dancing with him tonight?" she murmured. It was hard enough to think of Caleb with another girl, but the fact that he'd be with *Patience* was more than Malory thought she could handle.

She stayed with the gelding long enough to hug him and tell him he was the best horse in the whole world. Then she let herself back out of the stall, promising Tybalt she'd come see him tomorrow and tell him all about the formal.

As she jogged back to Adams House, Malory felt her stomach twisting with as many nerves as if she were about to ride in a competition. Even though Caleb was going to be with Patience that night, she couldn't push away her excited tension at the thought of being at a party with him. *This is crazy. I've got to accept that Caleb and I are just not right for each other and that he wants to be with Patience. It's time to move on*, she told herself as she ran up the staircase two steps at a time.

"At last!" Dylan exclaimed when Malory walked into the dorm. "We were about to send out the party police to search for you. Did you know you've only got three and a half hours to get ready?"

Malory didn't reply as she stared around the dorm room. It was a good thing Lynsey was getting changed in Patience's room. Every bed was covered in shoe boxes, underwear, makeup bags, blow-dryers, jewellry cases, and accessories.

The dressing table in the middle of the room was - designated for manicures and pedicures with a whole rainbow assortment of nail polish. On Dylan's desk were sodas, chips, and dips for them to keep up their energy while they got ready.

Dylan and Honey had already showered and were in their bathrobes with their hair wrapped up in towels. "Lani should be done, so you can hop into the shower any time," Honey told her.

Lani poked her head around the bathroom door. "Did I hear my name?"

"At last! I wouldn't be surprised if the water board announces a shortage. You'll be to blame when there's a sprinkler ban this summer," Dylan teased.

"Hey, by the end of the night there's going to be a whole load of boys willing to testify that the drought is worth it," Lani said.

"Well, in the dim light I guess they'll be forgiven

their mistake," Dylan fired back with a grin.

Malory left them to their banter as she went to get showered. Even the bathroom hadn't escaped the chaos and was littered with shampoos, conditioners, soaps, and exfoliators. It was like a sauna in there with the heat from three showers so far. Malory smiled as she noticed that Lani had drawn a heart in the steam on the mirror with the initials CH and SK, for the two boarding schools, in the middle.

She couldn't help thinking of how many hearts she'd sketched with her and Caleb's initials in them. "Right, that does it. That's absolutely the last time I'm thinking of Caleb tonight," she said out loud. Tonight was going to be all about celebrating the most amazing year at Chestnut Hill!

Malory decided to paint her nails baby pink to match her dress, which was one she'd worn for her end-of-year school party last year. Her allowance had stretched to having it lengthened and taken out, but a new dress had been out of the question.

She decided to wait until her nails dried before going to get her dress, a simple fit and flare. She hoped the others wouldn't think the colour was too childish. Her friends were unzipping their dresses out of plastic wrappers to hang in the bathroom. Honey had suggested doing this just in case there was the odd wrinkle that the steam would take out. Their dresses looked amazingly sophisticated as they shook them out.

"Are you going to open your present?" Dylan asked when she came back from the bathroom.

"I was planning on waiting until after we got ready," Malory replied. Just as she was leaving the show yesterday, her dad had given her a slim rectangular box. "Open it tomorrow night before the dance," he had told her.

"It might be a humongous box of chocolates," Lani said, her eyes lighting up.

"I'll go get it," Dylan said, ducking out of the door. She was back moments later with the ribbon-tied box, which she held out to Malory.

Putting the box down on Dylan's bed, Malory tugged at the ribbon and lifted off the lid. She parted the tissue paper.

"Dibs on the caramel!" Dylan said, coming to peer over Malory's shoulder.

Malory stared down at a sheath of blue silk in the box. Carefully, she picked it up and gasped as the folds dropped out to reveal a gorgeous dress.

"Wow," Dylan breathed.

Malory couldn't speak. It was the exact dress she'd admired in a shop window during her last holiday with her dad. He must have gone back and bought it for her as a surprise. Her throat tightened. He was the most amazing father ever. She knew that he'd have been hard-pressed to afford the dress but he'd done it anyway, knowing what it would mean to her. She spun around to show the dress to Lani and Honey.

Lani let out a low whistle. "You're going to look like

a million bucks in that. I might have to face up to losing some of my admirers to you."

"I'd say that's a given," Dylan warned. "Hang it up in the bathroom, Mal and I'll do your hair. Are you going to have it up or down?"

"I was going to go for down but I think a dress like this definitely needs it to be up," Malory said as she went to hang the dress on the curtain pole above the bathtub.

She sat on the stool by the mirror while Dylan began work on her hair. Now she knew how Cinderella must have felt when she was transformed from rags to riches.

"How's that?" Dylan sprayed a fine mist of hairspray over Malory's 'do and held up a mirror for her to be able to see the back.

Malory gently touched the cascade of ringlets that Dylan had curled and then twisted up on to her head. "It's amazing."

"Multi-talented, that's me." Dylan grinned.

"And a model of humility to us all," Honey teased.

Since she was the first to have her hair done, Malory figured she had time to slip down to the foyer to call her dad.

"Mal!" Her dad sounded surprised when he answered the phone. "I thought you'd be on your way to the dance."

"Soon," Malory told him. "I just wanted to say thank you for the dress. It's perfect."

"I'll bet you look beautiful in it," her dad said. "I wish

I could give you a wardrobe full of fabulous clothes."

"That's not important," Malory said. When you lost someone close, you realized that it was people that counted and not anything else. Caleb might think she was crazy for letting an opportunity like the riding programme pass by, but she knew she had her priorities straight. Her dad meant everything to her and being there for him wasn't a sacrifice, it was a privilege.

"I love you, Dad."

"I love you, too, sweetheart. Have a wonderful time tonight."

"I will," Malory promised. "I'll let you know everything that happens."

At six forty-five there was a knock on the door, and Mrs Herson looked in on them. "The vans are arriving," she said. "So if you're ready, you can make your way down to the foyer." She looked at the girls and smiled. "I think some hearts are going to get broken tonight."

"As long as they aren't ours!" Lani joked.

When their housemother closed the door, Dylan dramatically pressed her hand over her chest. "My heart's already been shattered by Henri."

Malory glanced at Dylan to check if her friend was OK despite her jocular tone. But Dylan was clearly enjoying herself.

"Hey, what would I do with an admirer on the other side of the Atlantic, anyway?" Dylan said as Malory continued looking at her in concern. "I'll get over it." She let out an overly dramatic sigh. "It may take some time. . ."

"Well, if your heart is shattered that leaves the field clear for me," Lani said. She reached for her shrug and slipped it over her bare shoulders. She was wearing an amazing off-the-shoulder red dress that stopped just above her knees, with a sheer overlay falling down to her calves.

"I said it was shattered, not out of commission," Dylan retorted. She picked up a small silver clutch purse that matched the colour of her Balenciaga bodice and skirt. "Are you guys ready?"

"Absolutely," Honey nodded, as she pushed one last pin into her hair. She'd put it into a French twist but left two tendrils to frame her heart-shaped face. Malory thought Josh would be bowled over when he saw how gorgeous his date was. Honey had gone for a classic black dress that set off her blonde hair and golden tan perfectly.

Before she followed the others out of the room, Malory took one final peek at her reflection. The dress was cut into a mock Grecian style with the blue silk skirt falling in soft folds to her ankles. Dylan had loaned her a pair of strappy Prada sandals, and Honey had dug out a twisted silver-and-gold rope necklace with matching earrings from her jewellry box. Malory barely recognized herself. She'd never dressed up like this before. *Thank you, Dad.* She picked up her purse and snapped off the light. The party hadn't even started and already it had been an amazing night.

Lani stood up inside the van and poked her head out of the window. Nobody else would join her for fear of spoiling their hair. "We're here," Lani said, sitting back down between Wei Lin and Honey.

Malory looked out of the window as the car swept up the gravel drive and drove around an ornate fountain. She loved the Saint Kits campus with its over-the-top, semi-Gothic architecture. The car pulled up outside the flight of stone steps leading to the main entrance. There were a few Saint Kits boys waiting at the top of the steps. Malory smiled when she recognized Josh looking really cute in his tuxedo. But then her heart missed a beat as she saw who was standing beside him. *Caleb!* He looked gorgeous with his dark hair combed and gelled, and the white shirt of his tux made his face seem even more tan than usual.

Razina nudged her. "The party isn't in the van, Mal. I think we have to get out."

"Sorry," Malory apologized as she realized they were waiting for her to open the door. She stepped out and wondered if there was any way she could possibly avoid seeing Caleb greet Patience. *No chance.* The second van carrying the remainder of the Adams seventh-graders pulled up behind theirs.

"Don't worry, we're with you," Dylan said in a low voice.

Malory tensed as Patience got out of the car, looking stunning in a dark red Vera Wang dress. She waved to Caleb and walked up the steps towards him. Lynsey walked beside her in her vintage Chanel dress. She smiled at her date, Jason Williams, who was waiting for her with a few of his friends.

"I take it you don't want to witness the big reunion," Lani said, coming to stand on the other side of Malory. It wasn't a question. She and Dylan marched her up the staircase talking loudly to block Malory from hearing Caleb and Patience greeting each other.

"That's gotta be the worst of it," Dylan reassured her. "From here on in, there's a huge crowd for us to get lost in." She pointed over the stone balcony that looked out over the lawn. It was covered by an enormous marquee that was strung with hundreds of bright lights. Music was pulsing from inside and already some of the Saint Kits boys were asking girls to dance.

"Come on, the steps go down to the lawn," said Lani. The staircase they'd just walked up ran along the side of the main building and then led down onto the grass.

"Malory!" Caleb was hurrying up the stairs behind them. "Wait up!"

Malory swapped glances with Dylan and Lani. "Do you want us to stay with you?" Dylan offered.

Malory hesitated. "No, it's OK, thanks. I'll catch up in a minute." She waited for her friends to start making their way down the steps before she turned to face Caleb. As she did, the butterflies appeared in her stomach once again.

"You look amazing," he said.

It wasn't what Malory had been expecting after their last talk. "Thanks. You look nice, too," she said, suddenly feeling shy. Then she remembered with a pang of sadness that she wasn't Caleb's date. She braced herself and went on, "Shouldn't you be with Patience?"

Caleb looked confused. "Why?"

"Well, you asked her to the dance, didn't you?" Malory reminded him.

Caleb opened his mouth and then closed it as Patience and Lynsey walked by. Lynsey was laughing at something Jason was saying. And Patience. . . Malory stared in astonishment. Patience was smiling up at a cute -eighth-grader who, judging by the way he had his hand possessively on her arm, was her date for the night.

"I didn't ask her!" Caleb said in surprise.

Malory frowned. "Um, I don't understand."

"Me, neither," Caleb said. "Sean planned on asking Patience to the formal a while ago."

"But Patience said *you* had asked her," Malory said.

Caleb shrugged. "Maybe Patience heard that someone from Saint Kits was going to ask her and assumed it was me. Does it matter?"

"I guess not," Malory admitted. "It would have been nice of her to have told me her mistake, though."

Caleb grinned. "Why, so you could ask me to be your date?"

"No!" Malory exclaimed in mock disgust.

"Why not?" Caleb pretended to look hurt.

"Because we're mad at each other," Malory told him. "Now if you don't mind, my friends are waiting for me." She left before he could reply, but as she hurried over to the marquee to join Dylan and Lani, she couldn't erase from her mind Caleb's look of hurt surprise as she'd cut short his friendly banter.

"What did he want?" Dylan immediately asked. Her eyes were wide with curiosity as she peeked over Malory's shoulder to stare at Caleb. "He doesn't look happy. What did you say to him?"

"Here," Lani held out a champagne flute of sparkling cider. "I got this for you."

"Thanks," Malory sipped the drink and looked around the tent, trying to gather her scattered emotions. The tent was fabulously decorated: potted plants stood in the four corners, the tallest touching the roof, which was swathed in folds of fabric and what seemed to be millions of tiny lights in the shape of stars. It was an evening for laughter and romance, not for accusations and arguments.

"Well?" Dylan prompted her.

"I told him we were still mad at each other," she groaned, regretting her hasty words.

"I'm not mad," Caleb's voice came from behind her. When she turned to face him, he gently took her drink out of her hand and gave it back to Lani. "I'm a jerk, maybe, but not mad." He smiled at Malory. "Did I tell you – you look amazing?"

"Yes," Malory replied, trying to keep her heart from turning somersaults as she felt her face get warm. She was uncomfortably aware of how close Caleb was standing and how handsome he looked in his tux. "But I don't mind you saying it again."

"Would you mind if I really pushed my luck and

asked you to dance?" The twinkle in Caleb's eye had nothing to do with the reflected sparkle of fairy lights.

Malory's heart was pounding so much that she knew Caleb had to hear it. "I guess that would be OK," she said, trying to ignore the matching grins on Dylan's and Lani's faces.

Caleb held out his arm and she felt a shiver run down her spine as she gave him her hand. She was feeling even more nervous than she had for their first date!

"I wanted to email you to say that I was being an idiot," Caleb told her as they walked onto the dance floor. Instead of moving to the beat like she'd expected, he held her arms and gazed into her eyes. "But I'm a guy, and admitting to being an idiot doesn't come easy." He gave her a slow, easy smile and Malory's heart flipped. "I shouldn't have reacted like that when you told me you weren't accepting the place in the programme. I know you think I've been totally wrapped up in competition since coming to school. I guess you've got a point. Winning is important to me, but there are other things that are important, too."

"Like what?" Malory could hardly believe what she was hearing. It was like time had reversed and she was talking to the boy she'd fallen for last summer.

"Like friendship," he said softly. "And horses! You've got a great partnership going on with Tybalt and competing for red ribbons doesn't have anything to do with it." He took a quick breath. "I've given it a lot of thought and I guess one of the reasons I was so mad at your decision not to go in the programme was because

I had been looking forward to the two of us spending time together." He looked down at his feet, his cheekbones darkening before he glanced back up. "Now look who you've left me to spend the holiday with: Lynsey Harrison!"

"Not long ago I'd have said you deserved each other," Malory said.

Caleb raised his eyebrows. "And now?"

"Now, I'm just enjoying our dance." Suddenly it was Malory's turn to feel awkward.

Caleb slipped his arm around her waist and began to move in time to the music. Malory moved with him and felt a rush of heady adrenaline as he whirled her around on the dimly lit dance floor. Josh was already dancing with Honey and as they spun by, Honey gave Malory a knowing smile. Whether it was because she was enjoying dancing with Josh, or because Malory was clearly back with Caleb, Malory couldn't tell.

Back with Caleb. The words repeated themselves over and over in her head.

Dylan and Lani joined them on the dance floor and began to make up some new steps in time to Madonna's latest track.

Dylan caught Malory's eye. "Is everything OK?" she mouthed.

Malory nodded at her friend as she rested her head on Caleb's shoulder. Everything was more than OK. Everything was just . . . *fabulous.*

Have you read the first story
in *Chestnut Hill?*

Chestnut Hill
The New Class

An extract...

"Dylan, we're almost there. Wake up, honey."

Dylan Walsh blinked her eyes open. Glancing out the window, she saw whitewashed fences lining lush green pastures. "What?" Dylan murmured. "Why'd you guys let me go to sleep?"

"We just got off the interstate a few minutes ago," her dad explained.

"You didn't miss anything." Dylan's mom looked over her shoulder into the backseat of the family SUV. "I thought you probably needed the rest."

Dylan rolled her eyes before she brushed her red hair behind her ears and turned her gaze back out the window. Dylan was relieved to know she'd soon be escaping her mother's overprotective ways. It was true that she hadn't been able to sleep a wink the night before. There had been too many things going through her head. She'd been looking forward to this day for so long – she was really on her way to Chestnut Hill! She searched the fields for any signs of horses, trying to gauge how close they were to the school. She wondered if all of Virginia was this picturesque.

Dylan followed the stretch of fence toward the horizon and her heart pounded when she saw the brick pillars that marked the entrance to the esteemed boarding school.

"This is it!" she yelled, recalling the first time she had visited the school. After the prospective-student weekend that spring, Dylan had been set on coming to Chestnut Hill.

She rolled down the window to get a better glimpse of the iron gates at the start of the drive. As her dad turned the car, Dylan's eyes focused on the Chestnut Hill crest. The chestnut tree (*what else?* she thought delightedly) with spreading roots and branches was worked into the ornate iron gate, along with the profile of a horse's head.

White rail fences continued on either side of the driveway, and Dylan shielded her eyes from the sun to scan the paddocks for the Chestnut Hill horses. She thought they were all beautiful, but she held her breath as she searched for one pony in particular.

Before she could find a familiar brown-and-white coat, the car turned to follow the gravel driveway, and the rest of the grounds came into view. Dylan leaned forward as they approached Old House, the magnificent white colonial building that had been the original school over one hundred years ago. With its tall white pillars, it gave Chestnut Hill a look of great Southern tradition. Now Old House just held faculty and administration offices, and the classrooms and science labs were in classic redbrick buildings on the other side of the campus. Ever since the fourth grade, when she read about it in *Horse and Rider* magazine, Dylan had wanted to attend Chestnut Hill for its top-tier riding programme. *I can't believe I'm actually here*, she thought, with a shiver of excitement. From the moment she had laid eyes on the campus that spring, she had been imagining this moment. Everything about the school was the best money could buy: the Olympic-size swimming pool, the indoor track, the art studio complete with ceramics workshop and kiln. And the school was known for high academic standards that prepared students for acceptance into the most competitive colleges, which pleased her parents.

Mr Walsh took a left turn, following the signs to the dorms on the north side of the campus. There were six houses, where students slept, studied, and generally hung out. Dylan already knew that she was in Adams House, which, very conveniently, was the dorm closest to the stable yard. She slid across the leather seat so she could look out the other window and tapped a drum roll with her fingers as they passed the wooden stables. *I'm going to be able to walk to the barn in less than five minutes*, she thought. *I'll be the most dedicated rider at Chestnut Hill. Just wait until team tryouts!*

Inside, a girl was carrying two buckets to the end stall. As the girl opened the door, Dylan caught sight of a magnificent black horse and twisted around so she could keep looking.

"Honey, you'll get whiplash if you keep turning your neck like that!" Mrs Walsh warned in a teasing tone.

Dylan straightened up, meeting her mother's eyes in the vanity mirror on the front passenger visor. "You need to brush your hair," Mrs Walsh told her. "It's flipping up again." She reached up to smooth her own neat red bob, but her tresses were already sleek and perfectly in place. Dylan might have inherited her mom's hair colour, but she sure didn't have the same patience to style and sculpt it.

"Maybe I'll just wear my hard hat." Dylan grimaced, running her fingers through her thick hair. "Then no one will notice." Her mom had been trying to persuade her to get a fringe, but she preferred having it all the same length, even if she needed a clip or a ponytail holder to keep it from falling into her eyes. "Hey, Dad, if you stop right now, I can get my hat out of the back."

Mr Walsh raised his eyebrows. "If we stop now, you'll disappear into the barn. Then you'd need a shower before you could pass your mom's inspection."

Dylan snapped her fingers. "You got me," she grinned. *Dad is so cool*, she thought, as she watched him pat her mom on the hand. *He totally gets me*. Her mom reached back and handed her a tortoiseshell hair clip. As Dylan reached for it, she switched off the DVD player built into the back of the front seat. She didn't mind not being able to watch the end of *Charlie's Angels*. Right now, real life was about one hundred times more exciting!

Dylan shifted to the middle of the backseat so she

could look out the front window. The road ahead was almost completely jammed with sports cars, SUVs, and luxury sedans. There didn't seem to be any parking spaces close to the dorm.

"Let's just stop here," Mr Walsh said, pulling over to the curb. "We can carry your luggage to the dorm."

Dylan had her hand on the door handle before her dad had even turned off the ignition. She jumped out onto the gravel path and took a deep breath. The air held a hint of autumn, but the sun, when it wasn't behind the clouds, was still at its summer strength. Everywhere Dylan looked, girls were getting out of cars, their arms full of garment bags and backpacks. Dylan followed her father around to the back of the SUV and pulled out the smaller of her two black suitcases. Mr Walsh let out a groan as he tested the weight of the larger bag.

"Come on, Dad. Here's your chance to prove what your country club membership does for you," Dylan said with a laugh. She doubted her dad had ever even been to the club's gym. He pretty much belonged for the golf and tennis, which he always ended up playing with his business partners. Without waiting to hear his reply, Dylan headed up the sidewalk in the direction of the dorms. She paused at the bottom of the sidewalk that led to the front door and tipped her head back to take in the white four-storey building. There were girls and parents on the steps leading up to the covered porch. Nobody had to wear the school uniform today, and everyone seemed to be taking advantage of that freedom. Like Dylan, lots of girls had on jeans and casual fitted tops, which was a relief. Dylan's mom had tried to get her to wear a pleated linen skirt with a cashmere tank, arguing that Dylan should try to make a good first impression.

The front porch cleared, and Dylan made her way up the steps and through the double doors. The foyer in Adams House seemed almost as busy as the unloading area outside and twice as noisy. Dylan caught her breath. In front of her, on either side of the room, was a formal double staircase that swept upward in a swoosh of crimson carpet. At the top of the stairs, a Chinese-style vase with a colourful and elaborate arrangement of flowers sat on a polished antique table. Sunlight streamed in through a beautiful stained-glass window on the second floor, making Dylan squint. *I feel like I'm in* Gone with the Wind, she thought. She hovered uncertainly, not having a clue where she should go.

"Excuse me!" An older student carrying a cello case stopped right in front of her.

"Oh, sorry," Dylan said, embarrassed, realizing she was blocking the door. She stepped to one side and placed her suitcase on the waxed hardwood floor. *Way to go, Walsh. No better way to look like a first-year student than standing right in the doorway with a dumb look on your face.* She took a deep breath and noticed a lovely scent of jasmine in the air. She tracked the aroma to another arrangement of flowers, this one in a cut glass vase on a polished maple table, the top of which was dappled with light. Dylan glanced up to see a magnificent chandelier hanging above her, dripping with crystals. She couldn't believe this was campus housing. It looked more like an interior design showcase.

"Dylan Walsh?" A smiling woman with dark curly hair appeared beside her. She glanced down at a clipboard and then back at Dylan. "Welcome to Adams House. Don't worry," she said. "This is the only day of the year when all chaos breaking loose is officially allowed." She held out her hand. "I'm Mrs Herson, your housemother. If you have any problems settling in, come see me and I'll try my best to help." Mrs Herson's brown eyes twinkled as she handed Dylan a map. "Noel Cousins, our dorm prefect, will show you where your room is, if you're ready."

"That would be great," Dylan said, reaching down for her suitcase.

Mrs Herson waved to a tall girl with wavy auburn hair who was just coming down the staircase. "Noel," she called. "This is Dylan Walsh. Can you take her up to Room Two?"

"Sure," the senior nodded, walking over.

"Noel is co-captain of the senior jumping team," Mrs Herson told Dylan. "So you already have something in common."

"Co-captain? That's great!" Dylan said, standing up a little straighter as she made eye contact with the senior. "I mean, isn't that what everyone wants? If they're in the riding programme, I mean." She winced. *What was going on?* Dylan was used to being so composed and knowing just what to say, but her words sounded all jumbled.

Noel smiled at the compliment. "I'd like to say it's not a big deal, but…"

"You don't want to lie, right?" Dylan relaxed enough to grin at the senior. She looked around for her parents, and, spotting them in the middle of the foyer, she waved for them to come over.

The Walshes followed Noel up the scarlet-carpeted staircase. Halfway up, the prefect paused and pointed down at a pair of doors leading off the foyer. "Before I forget, the seventh-grade common room and study hall are through there," she told Dylan. "I'm sure you'll log plenty of hours in those rooms."

As Dylan leaned forward to look down the corridor, a girl with her hair in cornrows started down the stairs, waving to someone below. She accidentally bumped against Dylan as she tried to get past. "Hey, watch it, Tanisha," Noel warned and gave Dylan an apologetic smile. "Typical upperclassman attitude. They forget they were rookies once, too!"

"I heard that," Tanisha called over her shoulder.

Listening to their banter Dylan bit her lip. Right now, it was hard to imagine she'd ever feel that comfortable around this place. It wasn't like her to be overwhelmed. She vaguely remembered her first day of kindergarten, and even then, she'd had a very practical, can-do attitude about taking on new things.

At the top of the stairs Noel turned left and walked down a hallway to a second, narrower flight of stairs.

"Your dorm room is up here," she explained. "You know, I started off in Room Two. I've always thought it's kind of lucky. Every year that I've been here, a first-year student from Room Two has made it onto the equestrian team."

"That's good news. I'm hoping to try out for the team," Dylan admitted, her heart beating faster.

"Yeah?" Noel glanced at her. "Competition's going to be tough this year, then. I know that Lynsey Harrison, who's rooming with you, is trying out, too." She paused to wait for Dylan's parents, who were looking rather out of breath. "Everyone gets used to all of the stairs after a while! There is a rickety elevator in the back, but Mrs Herson gives us a lecture on the importance of exercise if she catches us using it."

Noel held open the heavy fire doors at the top of the stairs, then led the way down a broad hall, past open doors where Dylan caught glimpses of girls unpacking. Her stomach flipped again as Noel stopped. This was it! Her room at Chestnut Hill!

"Welcome to Adams Room Two," Noel declared, opening the door. "You're rooming with Felicity Harper and Lynsey Harrison. You have a couple of hours to unpack and have a look around and then, at five o'clock, the school will be meeting in the chapel for our first convocation of the year." Noel stepped aside to allow Dylan to enter. "If you need anything, you can head down to Room Five. We're all seniors. We're a little more sane than the underclassmen. They'll calm down, though. It's just because it's the first day."

"Oh, it's OK," Dylan said. "I can handle a little insanity now and then."

"That's good to hear." A dimple flashed in Noel's cheek as she gave Dylan's parents a courteous smile. "Later," she said with a wave before slipping from the room.

Dylan let out a sigh. She hoped she had made a good impression.

Her mother stepped past her, hanging Dylan's garment bag over a chair. "Oh, this is lovely! Your lilac bedsheets will look fabulous against those floral drapes." She went over to feel the material. "You really lucked out."

Dylan followed her mom and looked around. There were three twin beds in the room, each with a matching cedar wardrobe and dresser with a pull-out desk top. The wood was the colour of warm honey, glowing in the sunlight that poured through the window at the far end of the room. It appeared that the bed immediately underneath the window had already been taken. Four cognac-coloured leather suitcases with the initials *LAH* were stacked next to it, and the bed itself was covered with shoe boxes and garment bags. Dylan set her own suitcase just inside the door.

Dylan's dad heaved the other bag over the threshold and straightened up, rubbing his back. "And I thought *you* packed too much. I pity whoever carried *her* luggage up those stairs," he joked, nodding toward the pile of bags by the window.

"That's right, Dad!" Dylan responded. "You should

never take me for granted. See what an easygoing daughter I am?"

"Yes, an easygoing daughter who begged incessantly for three years to go away to boarding school," her dad replied in a slightly accusatory tone.

Dylan knew that her father had wanted her to stay at home. She was an only child, and her dad had always treated her as though she were a friend as much as a daughter. They would swap jokes at dinner, go fishing on weekends, and, once in a while, go trail riding together. Dylan thought it was ironic – her dad had given her his love of horses, and that love had made her want to attend a boarding school over four hundred miles from home.

She walked to the far end of the room and leaned her elbows on the windowsill. The view looked straight across campus, but more importantly, it had a great view of the stable yard, where she could see a beautiful bay gelding being led in from the field.

"Look at the lines on that Thoroughbred. I bet he can really jump, huh?" Dylan's dad said as he joined her at the window. "I guess we would take him at Riverlea."

Dylan and her dad liked to daydream that they would buy a ranch out West and name it Riverlea. They'd have a dozen ponies and horses and then some cattle. Dylan knew it would never happen – for starters, she was more focused on equitation and jumping than riding Western and driving cattle – but it was fun to talk about. They sometimes did it just to tease Dylan's mom, who would consider moving to a ranch only if she could fly her hair stylist out weekly and get Prada home-delivered.

Mr Walsh pointed to a snazzy chestnut backing out of a trailer.

Dylan felt her stomach flip with excitement as she watched the everyday commotion of the stable: buckets, haynets, lead ropes, travelling wraps, horses, horses, horses! *Get me down there!* She couldn't wait to start pitching in. She'd spent most of the summer hanging out with her friends at the local stables, riding every day. Her instructor had let her try different mounts all summer, so it had felt as if she had half a dozen gorgeous ponies of her own. But the last few days had been filled with packing and sorting out her bedroom at home, so Dylan was anxious to get into the saddle again.

"Look at this set!" Mrs Walsh exclaimed, eyeing the suitcases on Dylan's roommate's bed and running her fingers over the largest one. "I'm sure I saw one just like it in Takashimaya on Fifth Avenue."

"They must belong to Lynsey Harrison," Dylan told her.

Mrs Walsh straightened up, beaming. "The Harrisons! Of course! I knew I'd heard the name. There was an article in *Vanity Fair* last month that mentioned Mrs Harrison's last fundraising event. The banquet was held at their home, and it was such a beautiful house. I'm sure Lynsey will make a wonderful friend for you, Dylan."

"Mom! Like I'd choose her as a friend because her

family has enough money to be featured in *Vanity Fair*!" Dylan said. *Why does mom always get so hung up on America's A-List?* She frowned.

Her dad held up his hands in a peacemaking gesture. "Whoa, I'm sure that's not what your mom meant. After all, any of the girls here are going to come from…" He looked left then right and dropped his voice to a whisper, "…moneyed backgrounds."

Dylan grinned and threw a pillow at him from the selection on the bed closest to her.

"Is that the bed you want, honey?" Mrs Walsh asked. "We'll help you unpack."

"Um, it's OK, Mom. I think I can handle it. Anyway, I thought I'd wait until Felicity arrives so we can see who wants which bed." *In other words, I'm ready for you to leave so I can go check out the horses,* she translated silently, catching her father's eye.

"Come on, hon. I'm sure Dylan can handle it. If we linger too long, she might actually think about how much she'll miss us. We don't want her to do that."

"Dad!" Dylan didn't want them to think she didn't want them around at all, but her urge to explore was too strong to suppress.

He caught her up in a huge hug, planting a kiss on the top of her head. "You have your cell phone, so be sure to call us if you need anything," he told her. "And even if you don't."

"Sure thing," Dylan replied, her voice muffled as she pressed her head into her father's shoulder.

She hugged her mom next and, as Dylan inhaled the

familiar Amouage perfume, a wave of homesickness gripped her. *This is going to be tougher than I thought.* It was going to be so weird being away from home for this long; this was way different from summer camp, where it was for just a few weeks, or from visiting her grandparents' house in the country. "Call us later," Mrs Walsh told her, reaching out to tuck a strand of hair behind Dylan's ear. "And don't forget your Aunt Ali is here for you."

"Yeah, right. Me and two hundred other girls," Dylan pointed out, but she smiled to show she was joking. Dylan hadn't known what to think when she had first heard that her aunt had taken over as Director of Riding at Chestnut Hill. Dylan's parents had already signed all her admittance paperwork, so it had been too late for her to change her mind. Dylan had always loved visiting Ali's stables in Kentucky, but this was different. She couldn't help but think that it would be awkward living on the same campus and having Ali as her riding instructor. *So much for my new independence!* Plus, Dylan didn't want the other girls thinking that she was going to get any favoritism from Ali. She wanted to make it at Chestnut Hill on her own. But right now, Dylan had to admit that the thought of a familiar face was sort of comforting. *Great. I'll be wanting a pacifier next.*

"I'll call later," she promised her parents. "Or you can call me when you get home." She walked to the door and watched them all the way down to the end of the hall. They turned and waved before disappearing through the double doors, and Dylan went back into the room. Suddenly it felt very empty. She sat down on the edge of the bed as a funny sensation, kind of like the butterflies she felt before a riding competition, hit her stomach. *Get a grip*, she told herself. *I'm at the best school in Virginia, which has an incredible riding programme, and my favorite pony in the whole world is waiting for me down in the stable.* She lay back on the bed and closed her eyes. She had a framed photo of Morello, the paint gelding, in her backpack, but she could picture him just as clearly in her head.

She'd first met him that summer when she'd spent a couple of weeks on her aunt's farm in Kentucky. Dylan smiled as she thought back to how quickly she'd become smitten with the pony. He had the cutest personality ever! He was adventurous and mischievous – Ali had said that Dylan and Morello had a lot in common. The first time Dylan had seen him, Morello had been loose in the stables, snuffling at the feed room door. Ali had quickly caught him and put him back in his stall, playfully reprimanding the pony as she slid home the bottom bolt. Morello could undo the top lock with his teeth, Ali explained. Then she told the story about the time he wandered up to the farmhouse and was caught pushing his way through the kitchen screen door.

Morello could be a challenge in the stable, but he was a dream in the ring. He had a great rhythmic pace, and his jumps exploded with energy. Dylan had never known a pony that made riding such fun.

And, while Dylan didn't want to flatter herself, she thought Morello had been just as taken with her. By the end of her stay, he would whinny whenever he saw her and come to her at the paddock gate.

Dylan's apprehension about Ali being accepted as the riding director quickly dissolved when she heard that Morello would make the move, too. Of course! He would be perfect for Chestnut Hill. And so would Ali. Her mom had made a big point about how this job was a great opportunity for Ali – a fresh start. Dylan knew her aunt was a talented instructor. Her students had dominated at the show they went to when Dylan was visiting.

Dylan thought about the photo of Morello in her bag. It had been taken at the Lexington Horse Show, where they had placed third in the Turnout class. Dylan had wanted to compete in a jumping class, but her mom insisted Ali would be busy enough with her regular students. Still, when Dylan claimed the yellow rosette, Mrs Walsh had acted like she'd won a ribbon at a major competition – and on reflection, Dylan thought she'd done pretty well to get Morello's white patches as clean as she had, and her braids were always neat and tight. Not all judges would rank a paint that high against all the stylish ponies at an A-level show.

Dylan looked up at the sound of the door opening. She felt her heart jolt as she prepared herself for the fact that her parents had probably come back for more good-byes. Instead, it was Noel Cousins who smiled in at her before stepping back to let a petite girl with shoulder-length blond hair enter the room.

Dylan stood up and helped the girl drag in her suitcases. "Welcome to Room Two!" she said, feeling like a veteran. Acting confident seemed to ease the butterfly battle in her stomach.

"Thanks." The girl smiled, pulling her hair back from her cute, heart-shaped face.

"Dylan, this is Felicity," Noel said. "I thought you could show her around. Just make sure you're both at the convocation."

"No problem." Dylan waited for Noel to shut the door behind her before turning to her new roommate. "How are you doing, Felicity?"

"I haven't been called that in ages," the girl replied, almost in a whisper. "It sounds so formal. You can just call me Honey."

Dylan blinked when she heard her new roommate's polished accent, but she didn't miss a beat. "Nice to meet you, Honey. I'm Dylan. I'm from Connecticut."

"Oh, I'm from ... well, I used to live in London, in England. We've only just moved out here – my father is a professor at the University of Virginia," Honey explained. She nodded toward the suitcases on the far bed. "Are they yours?"

"No!" Dylan said quickly. "They belong to Lynsey Harrison. I like to think of her as BBB."

Honey turned and raised a thin blond eyebrow.

"Best Bed Bagger," Dylan translated, her face

perfectly straight. "I mean, I guess it's first come, first served, so I don't really blame her."

Honey smiled. "So we get to choose between the other two, then?"

"You go first, I'm cool with either one."

"Well, if you're sure you don't mind, I'll take this one." Honey pointed to the bed nearest the door. She skirted Dylan's bed and lifted up a stylish plaid backpack. She unzipped the front pocket and pulled out a stack of photographs.

"Hey, he's gorgeous!" Dylan exclaimed, spotting a picture of a showy chestnut pony jumping over parallel bars. "Is he yours?"

"He was," Honey confirmed with a wistful sigh. "His name's Rocky. My parents bought him for me when I was nine, but I had to leave him in England." Honey reached out to trace her finger across the glass in the photo frame.

"That must have been really hard," Dylan said sympathetically. She had never had a pony of her own, but she knew how difficult it had been saying goodbye to Morello after riding him for only two weeks.

She figured it would be kind of rude to head straight for the stable yard now that Honey had arrived. She started to unpack, almost wishing she had taken her parents' offer to help as she realized just how much she had brought with her – her school uniform, riding stuff, clothes for wearing around the dorm, clothes for formal dinners, not to mention books and photos. And at the bottom of the case, there was a stuffed panda bear named Pudding that her grandmother had knitted when Dylan was a baby. He was a bit squashed after being stuffed in the oversized suitcase, but she gave him a shake, pummeled his nose back into shape, and propped him on her pillow.

Honey glanced over and caught her eye. For a moment Dylan paused. *Is it totally babyish bringing a stuffed bear to boarding school?* But then Honey wordlessly took out a small brown bear and tucked him under the top of her duvet, before flashing a grin at Dylan.

"There was no way I was coming here without Woozle!" she joked.

Relaxing, Dylan unwrapped the layer of tissue paper from around the first photograph. It showed her dad holding up a sign for his engineering company's new branch, with his other arm around Dylan's mom. The next photo was one of Dylan standing next to Morello, the yellow ribbon clipped to his bridle.

"Oh, do you ride, too?" Honey asked, leaning over to look. "What a fabulous pony!"

"This is Morello. He's actually here at Chestnut Hill. He's a little spoiled. He'll probably expect a bunch of organic carrots off a silver platter when he sees me," Dylan told her. "I was about to go down to the stable before you got here. Do you want to head down together?" She glanced at her watch. "We've got lots of time before convocation."

Honey's brown eyes lit up. "That sounds good."

Dylan grinned, figuring things couldn't get much better – and she'd only been at Chestnut Hill for an hour. She sprang to her feet. "Let's go!"